Porgy & Bess
By
Miles Davis
By
George Gershwin
By
Dubose Heyward

Jeffrey DeShell

SPUYTEN DUYVIL

New York City

Library of Congress Cataloging-in-Publication Data

Names: DeShell, Jeffrey, author.
Title: Porgy & Bess by Miles Davis by George Gershwin by Dubose Heyward / Jeffrey DeShell.
Description: New York City : Spuyten Duyvil, [2022]
Identifiers: LCCN 2022030177 | ISBN 9781956005691 (paperback)
Subjects: LCGFT: Detective and mystery fiction. | Novels.
Classification: LCC PS3554.E8358 P67 2022 | DDC 813/.54--dc23/eng/20220624
LC record available at https://lccn.loc.gov/2022030177

On Jeffrey DeShell

Masses and Motets
Jeffrey DeShell has managed to make the form of the crime novel erudite, challenging, and entertaining at the same time. What a wonderful *trompe l'oeil*, a true literary experiment and adventure. This is a truly fine piece of work.
  Percival Everett

The Trouble with Being Born
In *The Trouble with Being Born*, the parents trade riffs, mother and father telling their stories in short, staccato sentences. Jeffrey DeShell's writing of them gets under the skin, the way parents' "autobiographies" also live under their children's lives. DeShell is a daring, intelligent, hard-eyed, and tenderhearted writer, all of which is abundantly evident in his wonderful new novel.
  Lynne Tillman

Arthouse
An avant-noir tour de force, Jeffrey DeShell's *Arthouse* is an architecturally stunning exploration of how we are all thought by cinema. Peopled by tweakers, dealers, killers, a woman hostage, and an ex-con academic, set in a blasted corner of the New West, and shot through the lenses of fourteen films, this extraordinary novel appropriates and celebrates a multiplicity of filmic vocabularies and points of view, even as it turns family into a Fellini, sex into a Suzuki, and the world into a series of eccentric angles, incommensurate scripts, and beautiful, stylized, joco-serious, self-reflexive textual double exposures.
  Lance Olsen

To Marco Breuer

You want me to do what I said

You certainly heard me he said I certainly said it loud enough he said for you to certainly hear but for the sake of peace he said for your sake and the sake of peace I'll repeat myself something I generally prefer avoiding he said but I do want you to understand he said I said I want you to go to Boulder I want you to investigate the alleged shooting he said the alleged shooting by the Boulder police officer I'm sure you know what it is I'm talking about the alleged shooting of a student in one of the university dormitories by the Boulder police officer he said they've asked us to help he said the Boulder District Attorney has asked for our help he said has asked us to provide an independent investigator to provide an independent investigation the investigator unbiased unencumbered by familiar professional relationships he said they've asked for you specifically he said for you specifically to go to Boulder to conduct this independent investigation this outside inquiry this nonbiased look into this alleged shooting of a university student in one of the university dormitories he said to lead something called their Critical Incident Team they've asked for you specifically he said and I've agreed and so you should leave for there he said as soon you leave here

This is such a bad idea for so many reasons I said a really terrible idea for so very many reasons too many to count I said too many reasons to count it would take an hour or two just to begin to total up the very many reasons this is such an absolute mistake I said but to get the ball rolling I said I'd like to offer an introduction not to the counting of the reasons but an introduction to the reasoning of the first of the reasons itself I said and the first of the reasons itself I said is the question of jurisdiction the Colorado Bureau of Investigation this is their job and by their job I don't mean that it is a task they can choose to do or not but it is rather a job they were designed to do I said in fact their very existence is based on this very type of job this very type of job of outside investigation this very type of job of unbiased inquiry this very type of job of a Colorado police department requiring external eyes to scrutinize and analyze the Colorado police themselves I said this very type of job when the police are being policed when investigators are being investigated is the *raison d'etre* of the Colorado Bureau of Investigation I said so the first of these reasons why this is such a bad idea to send me to Boulder as an outside investigator to investigate the shooting of an unarmed black university student by an officer of the Boulder Police Department is the fact that such an agency already exists in order to do that very outside investigative job this reason is so substantial and unarguable I said it should immediately disqualify further consideration of the bad idea project

You need to watch your language he said

You're right I said I apologize

I am your superior officer and I will not be addressed in such a disrespectful manner

You're right I said I apologize

You will be going to Boulder he said

I will explain myself further he said even though I owe no further explanation as your superior officer he said I can simply order you to accept the Boulder assignment to investigate the alleged shooting and by simply I mean merely without further explanation or justification I need merely state my orders that you accept the Boulder assignment and then you'd be obliged by your duty as we both understand it as the entire Denver Police Force understands it as most if not all Denver civilians understand it to accept my order and take the Boulder assignment nothing else on my end is required he said so if I proceed further along the explanation path it is not something owed you he said but something I am doing because by proceeding further down the explanation path I believe I might help you complete the Boulder assignment more skillfully he said more skillfully and perhaps more quickly he said in a more timely manner which is what we both desire he said a job done quickly and well he said would be to everyone's advantage

Yes I said

The Boulder District Attorney would prefer not to involve the Colorado Bureau of Investigation because the Boulder District Attorney believes the Colorado Bureau of Investigation to be should we say he said compromised when it comes to investigating situations involving local police departments *vis a vis* racial and sexual minorities he said the Colorado Bureau of Investigation's track record is the opposite of exemplary or if it is exemplary it's certainly bad exemplary a negative exemplary he said and above all he said well perhaps not above all but above most on the list he said the Boulder District Attorney wants everyone to see that the Boulder District Attorney is conducting an undeniably impartial and unquestionably fair investigation the Boulder District Attorney as well as the Boulder Police Department want there to be absolutely no taint of whitewashing or police coverup in this alleged shooting he said the utmost transparency were the words they used he said which is why they came to us and yes he said before you ask the Colorado Attorney General has agreed he said the Colorado Attorney General has agreed that utmost transparency is of critical importance and the Colorado Attorney General also agrees that there would be no issues assigning you a temporary transfer to the Boulder Police Department so as far as your initial objection there is in fact nothing there there is there anything else he said

They approached you I said but why me I said

I've already answered your question he said I don't know why you're pretending ignorance he said the particulars of this alleged shooting are well known impossible to avoid he said you must realize given the particulars of the alleged shooting and given the particulars of the Boulder District Attorney's desire for utmost transparency that you would be not only an appropriate investigator but even the most appropriate investigator he said of all the possible investigators known you are the one that best fits the most appropriate box

Because I'm a woman I said

Because I'm a white woman I said

Your refusal to answer is an answer I said

I'm being sacrificed I said

Elissa please have Lieutenant Clark join us as soon as possible he said

Calling in reinforcements I said

Lieutenant Clark has a better grasp of the language of such assignments he said and perhaps can provide clearer insight with his Boulder assignment language grasp and besides he said I understand the two of you have developed something of a rapport

We have no rapport I said

Lieutenant Clark you know Detective Fruscella

Of course good to see you Detective he said

We are all here on a Saturday I said

Detective Fruscella has a few questions about the Boulder assignment he said the alleged shooting of the minority student in the university dormitory he said

Yes he said

It's not an alleged shooting I said the shooting was real there's nothing alleged about the fact that a young man was shot

Detective I've warned you he said

And killed I said

No he said she's right he said that's one of the aspects of the case that is beyond dispute a young man was shot by a Boulder police officer and is now deceased no one is arguing that he said

It makes me nervous when you take my side I said

Why he said

An African American student was shot and killed by a white woman police officer in Boulder Colorado I said is there anything alleged in what I just said I said

No he said

No he said

And I'm a white woman police detective is there anything alleged about that I said

And so the Boulder District Attorney and the Boulder Police Department are aware enough to know that for anyone to believe this is on the up and up that this is transparent they need to bring in someone external and for anyone to believe this is on the up and up and absolutely transparent the someone external they do bring in can't be from the Colorado Bureau of Investigation so they contact you and ask for me I said knowing that by not being from the Colorado Bureau of Investigation I'll look appropriate and they'll look good good and transparent what's a clearer way of saying this Clark

Targeted optics

Targeted optics oh that's beautiful targeted optics so by not being from the Colorado Bureau of Investigation I said they optically target the African American community and by being a Caucasian woman I said they optically target the white Boulder community not to mention police everywhere especially the unions I said and those Weld County yahoos and Springs fascists who'd give their right nuts to go to Boulder and crack some libtard skulls and get all rapey with the ski chicks and here I am I said the stone killing the two birds I said all dressed up like Norma atop her pyre or Tosca in her castle you have no idea what I'm talking about neither of you do you

No he said

No clue he said

By insisting on me rather than Detective Royal I said or Captain Hixon who made Captain because of his homicide work let alone that hot shot African American in Pueblo Crimes Against Persons Unit what's his name

Chambers

Yeah Chambers so why not Chambers and why me I'll tell you why they pick a woman I'll spell it out they think hope that I'll have natural sympathy for this white woman officer some unconscious chromosomal slash melaninal bond I said I mean what white woman hasn't felt threatened by a black guy right and so I'll find enough to secure an indictment any indictment I said a Boulder grand jury will have to indict else the entire county will be put off its kale but as far as a murder charge no way she's a cop she's white and she's a she I said and notice I said we're still talking indictment not even conviction I said the most I see here is a six month suspension with pay and what with qualified immunity she can't even get sued for damages so what's the problem you ask I said I'll tell you I said what happens when I come back here I said whatever indictment the Boulder District Attorney settles on will be a compromise I said too little for some too much for others for the too little crowd I'll be just another white woman racist yelling rape at the slightest negro glance for the too much crowd I'm crossing that thin blue line betraying my brothers and sisters selling out to the PC terrorists I said so to put it politely I lose either way and for what I said for what

It's not like that he said not like that at all

You're misreading the situation Detective you're a decorated detective with a reputation for fairness and rigor he said

Soon to be sacrificed on the altar of absolute transparency and targeted optics and for what I said so the I don't see color sanctuary city can wash its lily white hands of anything resembling unpleasantness or even the most basic acknowledgement that life is fucking unfair I said talk about your buzzkill I said talk about ruining your *namaste* I said no I don't want to do it I said I really don't want to do it I said

The minutes spent complaining you and explaining me haven't moved the needle in the slightest he said the Boulder assignment remains unchanged unchanged both in the sense that the actual assignment of investigating the alleged shooting of an African American student by a Boulder Police Officer has not altered as well as in the sense he said that the person originally assigned this Boulder investigation despite her various reservations and resistances bordering on insubordination remains assigned to the Boulder investigation he said part of the fault he said with the expenditure of these minutes is mine I readily admit in the interest of camaraderie efficiency and general *l'esprit de corps* he said I agreed to follow a path of explanation but I've now come to realize he said that by following this path of explanation this slightly indulgent path of forced camaraderie I've given the impression the mistaken impression that this path of indulgent explanation might evolve or somehow lead up to a place of actual discussion this was never a possibility he said it was never a possibility to reach anything resembling a point of actual discussion it was always only ever a path of explanation so we've wasted your time he said by following down this false path your time he said as well as mine

If I may add Detective that given the unrest now trending a quick and visual response is vital

Couches will get burned candles lit and petitions signed not feeling the urgency I said

Aren't you interested in finding out what happened he said

I know what happened I said

Aren't you the least bit curious he said about what really happened Captain do you have the case file handy

It's pulled up on my computer he said

Listen to this I'm reading the Boulder police report he said on November twenty seventh at ten forty nine PM the Boulder Police Department received a call from the University of Colorado Police Department asking them to investigate a trespassing slash possible break in on the third floor of the Arnett Residence hall he said there's a note here stating that CUPD was busy with the traffic and quote busting drunks at the football game unquote

I don't want to hear it I said

Officers Shields and Robbins responded immediately arriving at the main entrance at approximately eleven oh two we took the elevator to the third floor and when we arrived we identified ourselves and observed the suspect a Mr Johan Alexander Ratcliff behaving erratically and belligerently staggering around the commons area he appeared intoxicated he said Officer Shields began to try to calm him he said when Ratcliff turned ran down a hallway and disappeared into one of the bedrooms we Shields and Robbins attempted to follow but Ratcliff locked the door he said Shields heard scuffling noises as she knocked on the door repeatedly demanding Ratcliff open the door after three or four minutes Robbins proceeded downstairs to obtain a master key or some help opening the door while Robbins was gone Ratcliff opened the door he said

Enough I said

And began to approach Officer Shields he said in a quote threatening and abusive manner unquote and that Ratcliff quote was brandishing a large stone object in his right hand unquote Shields retreated and repeatedly ordered Ratcliff to stop and drop the stone but Ratcliff did not comply nor did he slow or hesitate as he proceeded down the hallway he said toward Officer Shields Ratcliff continued his abusive and threatening manner and quote Ratcliff lunged at Shields knocking her down unquote

All right I said all right who's their lead detective

Name of Goldsmith

I know Goldsmith I said he's a cowboy

Officer Shields felt she was in imminent danger of bodily harm so she discharged her weapon three times hitting the assailant in his shoulder chest and neck he said

Goldsmith's statement and witness statements are

pending as well as a preliminary coroner's report he said Ratcliff was pronounced dead at twelve fifty six AM he said by one doctor Nelson bloodwork and tox reports pending

Who called it in I said

A resident of the dormitory a Ms Nancy Belhomme of Longmont

And who was in the room with Ratcliff

A Ms Serena Frazier KNBC reported she was his girlfriend

He was spending the night with his girlfriend when some sheltered Suzy saw this black stranger wandering in the commons clutched her pearls and dialed nine one one I said

This is way fucked I said

Priors he said

This is way fucked I said

Pending he said

And Goldsmith that's just perfect I said

So Detective he said you're still here

I know Goldsmith I said

So you said he said is that a problem

Could be

No it couldn't be he said couldn't possibly be look he said all you've done here today is to take this personal

Personally

And personal he said doesn't work with professional this conversation has gone on for far too long he said Detective I expect you in Boulder by noon today you're to report to a Captain Christian

So I don't have a choice

Notice my smile Detective of course you have a choice he said you can report to Captain Christian by noon today or you can go home and relax while this office prepares your severance package

It's completely your choice he said

Detective Fruscella he said I'm grateful you've agreed to help us

Captain Christian I said

How was the drive up Thirty Six can be difficult he said what with all the construction

It was fine I said not much traffic the mountains are pretty

Students are gone for Thanksgiving break he said DIA will be a madhouse tomorrow please sit down would you like some coffee

No thank you I said lucky for you I said

Lucky for me what he said

Students out of town I said until things cool down

Ah so you heard the protests on the way in yes the vocal minority like I said he said the students are home for break not sure who the loudmouths are a few bad apples he said a few bad apples plus outside agitators from Denver would be my guess but we're here to protect their rights too as long as nothing gets broken he said Boulder County sheriff will help us out if need be he said and I play tennis with the Longmont and Louisville captains so same deal there police work's all about cooperation he said I think we're good to go he said no need to worry

I wasn't worried

And the football team won he said

I emailed your Captain Schlaff the case file to forward

on to you he said we now have a more detailed preliminary coroner's and a number of witness statements he said we are still waiting on the transcript of Goldsmith's interview the DA whom you'll report to should be contacting you later this afternoon let me make sure I have your email I'll cc your captain but no need to route it all through the Denver office if your captain's inbox is anything like mine he might appreciate being initially status ignorant

Procedures were followed I said weapons sequestered clothing isolated Gun Shot Residue tested

By the book he said strictly by the book we don't want any questions regarding the rigor and scrupulousness of our evidence gathering and chain of custody procedures he said we want to need to he said treat the unfortunate death of this young man with the utmost fairness and objectivity and the only way to do this he said is to follow the book as meticulously as possible he said we need to keep everything and I cannot stress this enough he said we need to keep everything above suspicion he said and this obviously includes you and your investigation he said absolutely above any and all suspicion

And where do I come in I said

Didn't Captain Schlaff brief you he said

He did but unfortunately what he says I said and what I hear I said sometimes differ

That doesn't reflect well on you Detective he said

No not at all I said but this case is too important to allow initial assumptions or preliminary miscommunications to perhaps obscure or cloud the facts of the case

That's true he said although the passive voice is misleading

Let me put it this way I said in order for me to be as completely and unequivocally fair and objective as I can possibly be I need to know exactly and precisely why you requested me I said why you thought I said that I rather than any other detective from the Denver Police Force would be the most likely to provide the fair and objective investigation you require

It wasn't my idea he said it was the District Attorney's

So I'm here without your approval I said

Don't be dense Detective of course you're here on my approval although I believed and still believe that this is a case best left to our own Internal Affairs Unit protocol insists that we convene a special Critical Incident Team to provide outside eyes on the case and the outside eyes in this case that's you

But why my eyes in particular

You have a stellar reputation Detective he said you handled the Benderson case with rigor and discretion and that priest murder dear Lord he said what are we coming to he said anyway we the DA and I thought that a high profile decorated detective like yourself would go a long way he said a very long way to keeping this investigation transparent and above suspicion he said you were he said our first choice he said our only choice

And the Colorado Bureau of Investigation

Decided against he said given the Allison case and the Jenson case and other cases previous we concluded the CBI could not provide the necessary transparency he said would not provide the necessary objectivity he said I explained this all to your captain and I'm surprised he didn't pass this on to you or if he did he said I'm surprised you didn't think enough of it to retain

Given your cooperation with local police departments why didn't you bring in a detective from one of those surrounding L towns Louisville or Longmont what's the other

Lyons he said as you know Detective Lyons and Louisville are much too small to require or support a homicide division Longmont has a Crimes Against Person unit but that's all Denver is the only place in the state where folks kill other folks with any regularity he said nowhere else well maybe Pueblo once in a while Vail and Aspen mostly OD.

JonBenet was before your time I said

So you asked for me initially and Schlaff agreed I said

Your captain agreed readily

And you asked for no one else I said

No he said you were our first and only choice

How important I said was my gender to your decision

I'm afraid I don't understand he said

I'm trying to determine what role I said my gender played in establishing that I would be your first and only choice I said to lead this transparent and objective investigation

I still don't understand he said

I trying to be as clear as I possibly can be I said I need to know why out of all the possible homicide detectives in the state you focused on me a woman was it the me or was it the woman I said which was the deciding factor I said let's say the woman and the me are inseparable can't have one without the other then what do you gain by having me and what do you gain by having a woman and which the me or the woman might be more important we don't I said have to necessarily fix a ratio a percentage I said say fifty per cent me fifty per cent woman or sixty slash forty whatever I said no what's more important than the ratio is the reasoning behind it the supposition or to be more precise the presupposition although that is not really precise given that that difference between presupposition and supposition is non existent I said what was or rather is the supposition of the function of my gender in investigating this case I said is my gender supposed to function as a sort of focal point a site of optics targeted or not I said where an external uninvolved objective investigator is seen to have her objectivity tempered by her gender tempered by the care and concern her gender signifies so that her cold blooded objective detachment co exists with a warm womanly empathy and even possible sympathy for the accused although she's not accused I said not yet perhaps not ever and this split personality this ambivalence this complexity this detached yet sympathetic examination and analysis this objective sympathy or we could just as easily say sympathetic objectivity is visible for everyone both public and police I said it's this ambivalence this give and take that creates the appearance of fairness there's another supposition possible I said a more internal supposition and that internal supposition supposes that there does exist a real and natural connection between two women I said in this case the investigator and the possibly accused I said a connection if not based on gender and experience then certainly *strengthened* by gender and experience this supposition implies that there will be a genuine sympathy between the investigator and possibly accused and that this sympathy will likely if not in fact color the investigator's examination and analysis and will likely if not in fact determine the outcome of the investigation so you see I said I need to know if what you're thinking was or is along these lines

Schlaff warned you were difficult he said insubordinate and stubborn

I suppose I can live with the supposition I said that women are naturally or culturally generous I said although anyone who knows me knows I'm not at all warm and fuzzy I said the word bitch is used often I said around me

I thought he may have been exaggerating but I can see that he wasn't

It's the second supposition that I object to I said the supposition that implies shared gender equals shared experiences and therefore shared thinking

Your attitude could make working here he said challenging we pride ourselves on the inclusivity and diversity of our department he said we also pride ourselves on our cohesiveness we tend to get along here Detective

I will not allow the shared gender supposition I said and the supposed shared experiences supposition I said to color and therefore destroy the investigative objectivity I said which would be to destroy the investigation itself I said if I'm going to do my job I said I'm going to do it as best I know how I said

Inclusivity and diversity require recognition of structure he said

So if that was your intention I said it's a supposition I do not recognize and I said it's a supposition I cannot abide

Recognition and adherence to structure he said otherwise all is chaos and confusion

It may not have been a conscious decision

The District Attorney fastened on you and I agreed perhaps my agreement was hasty

I'm not accusing anyone of deliberately or consciously establishing my gender as the primary criteria guiding the choice to name me the investigator I said and to bank on as it were a sympathetic gender connection between the object of this investigation and myself I said as any such conscious assumptions suggesting those of similar professions and similar genders naturally share similar experiences which then naturally or culturally imply similar attitudes and reactions I said are outdated to say the least

Would you like to meet your team he said

Especially in somewhere as progressive as Boulder I said

Sergeant Jones will be your liaison and guide Officer Carter will handle data and Officer Williams will help with interviewing Officer Shields is suspended for the foreseeable he said and at home but I believe Detective Goldsmith is around

But a supposition doesn't need to be conscious to

influence I said a supposition can float around vague and unspoken but extremely strong for all that I said or not float around necessarily but actually anchor establish the very foundation of subsequent thoughts and actions I said sometimes it's the unthought unspoken unconscious suppositions I said which are in fact the most persuasive sometimes it's the unthought unspoken suppositions I said which in fact are the ones most difficult to shake you can't shake an anchor I said

Sergeant Jones this is Detective Fruscella from the Denver Police Department

Not to mention color or race I said a white woman investigating another white woman

Detective Fruscella this way please he said

All I'm saying I said is that it is my intention I said to be objective and fair to both perpetrator and victim although at this moment it's impossible to determine which is which and that any supposition thought or unthought to the contrary I said for whatever reason I said is a mistaken supposition pure and simple

We're in Situation Room C it's the smallest but we have a drug operation going with DEA so they get the A and B this is Officer Carter she'll be helping with data and technical

Detective she said

High tech impressive I said hello

And this is Officer Williams

I'll do the running around for you Detective

Williams I said

I'll let you all get to work

Let's go through the entire file shall we feel free to add to my knowledge did the other officer what's his name give a separate report

Robbins

Yes Robbins did Officer Robbins file a separate report

No Detective

Where's the hard copy of this file I said I'm tired of looking over your shoulder ah thank you did Goldsmith interview Officer Robbins I said

Says here Goldsmith scheduled an interview with himself Robbins and Detective Sullivan at three forty five this morning she said

Where's the recording of the interview

Should be stored in the evidence drive do you want to look at it she said

Soon I said

The vic does have a record shoplifting one count one count possession one count jaywalking

Jaywalking I said where was that

Here she said Boulder

You bust people for jaywalking I said seriously I said

Shoplifting Nederland two years ago liquor store said he boosted a bottle of cognac

Plea

Not guilty charges dropped

What about the cop Shields

What about Shields

Any record any formal complaints anything from Office of the Independent Monitor

What's that

Office of Independent Monitor don't you have that here

Professional Standards Unit and then IA she said but no no complaints listed

Any use of force since she's been here

None listed

What about previous jobs I said

Police Academy in Colorado Springs graduated 2009 worked in the Springs PD 09 to last February when she started working here

You know her I said

No she said

I know her from sight he said but we've never talked

No he said

Any record of complaints in the Springs

Nothing in her file he said

Anyone know who her friends are who she hangs out with why she moved out here she married have a boyfriend girlfriend I said

Nothing in the file he said

I want to know more about her I said is her partner around Robbins I said

Yes he's on a desk until the review's concluded

Where can I see him on the desk

Ask the DO he said

I think she said he's on Evidence

Where's that I said

Down the hall to your right she said

Do you want some help he said

Sure I said and you can please cue up the Goldsmith interview I said I'll watch it when I return

Officer Robbins I said I'm Detective Fruscella and you know Sergeant Jones I believe

Detective Sergeant

I've been brought in from the Denver Police Department to head up an investigation into the shooting last night and I'd like to ask you a few questions about what happened I said I know you were formally interviewed by Detective Goldsmith and I haven't had the chance to look at that interview I only have a couple of questions now though I said is there someplace we go could for a few minutes can you get someone to take over I said

I already talked to IA

Internal Affairs is running their own investigation I still need to talk to you

I can call in Rawlings he said

Thank you Officer it will only take five minutes where can we go Jones

We can use an interview room I think Two is open

Two it is then I said

Please sit down Officer I only have a couple of questions I'm trying to get a handle on Officer Shields before I formally interview her I said can you give me any information about her what she's like I said what she likes to do I said whom she hangs out with anything like that I said

I don't know her that well he said

How long have you been partners

Couple of months he said

She's been here since last February I said that's nine

months ago

I wasn't her first partner here he said we've only been partners since August

How often do you rotate partners here

We don't usually rotate assignments he said

It's all part of this community policing initiative he said

Who was her partner before you

Forsythe

Is this usual Jones I said partners splitting after a couple of months

Not usual but it happens he said

She say why she split with Forsythe I said

No he said

You ever ask

No he said

Was it that it never occurred to you or was it that it was clear that she didn't want you to ask

I got the definite impression she didn't want to talk about it

What did you talk about I said

Working out he said running lifting that sort of thing he said she's big into crossfit he said kettleballs and I do ironman

Did you ever go to the gym together

Once in a while when we started he said maybe twice a month maybe less not so much lately he said

Why not I said

She was getting more into yoga and I don't know

What

I got the feeling she liked working out with other gals

Oh

Some girls are like that they don't want guys checking them out or something I don't know

Did you check her out I said

No he said I have a girlfriend and you know we work together that can be trouble he said

Do you know any of the women she did work out with

She told me about these women he said from the Sheriff's department and Boulder Fire he said

Did you see her socially other than working out I said did you ever go for a drink or anything

We never went out he said I went to her apartment once for a party

And

I had a couple of beers talked to some of her friends some girls from Colorado Springs some girls from Broomfield good looking friends he said fitness models and the like

But aside from a few workouts and that party you didn't see Shields socially

That's right

Last night why did you leave to go unlock the door

That hallway he said was narrow that's one of those old dorms barely room to turn around we were trying to handle it with the least possible noise you know the least possible hassle

Why didn't she go and you remain with the suspect

She just happened to be there first Detective no other reason just the way it happened we would have had to get all twisted around to switch places he said and besides he said no way she would have agreed she'd have felt dissed

After Ratcliff retreated into the dorm room you didn't see him until you returned after hearing the shots is that correct

That's right

And how long was that between the shots and when you returned

A couple of minutes I guess I had to run up two flights of stairs

And Ratcliff was wounded and bleeding when you saw him correct

That's right

Did he have that rock in his hand that bookend I said

He did he said

And he's gripping it tight

I guess so he said

I mean it was in his hand I said it wasn't loose by the body or anything

No it was in his hand he said

Was it loose in his hand like just on his palm I said or were his fingers around it

I'm not sure Detective

And where was Shields when you came up

I didn't see her at first he said but she was in the dorm room searching the room

How was she I said

Detective he said

Shields was she flustered upset shaken

Not really he said she was professional like always

And then you tried to help Ratcliff yes

I did Detective he said

Was Ratcliff conscious I said responsive

No he said not at all I got a weak pulse but he was bleeding out pretty good

Thank you Officer I said thank you

BOULDER POLICE HEADQUARTERS

I've got more info on Ratcliff he said Detective

And Detective Goldsmith is looking for you

Ratcliff attends attended CU Boulder as a graduate student he said and get this he was a graduate student in philosophy he was active in something called the Black Existentialists I'm going to call CUPD now and see if they have a file he said Black Existentialists they call themselves BE

What sport did he play he said

Where'd you go to school I said existentialism was sexy those French guys in berets smoking cigarettes not exactly a threat except for the cigarettes call the philosophy department then follow up with the university police

Detective

Detective Goldsmith

It's been a long time Detective

Yes it has looks like Boulder's treating you well

Can't complain Fruscella can't complain I read about you in the papers he said a commendation from Homeland Security and a Denver Police whatever he said not too shabby you always were ambitious he said

Yeah I'm so lit they send me here I said

Not so bad here he said good restaurants fresh air clean living all good except for the drugs

And the occasional rape I said

Least we're not killing priests in church he said

Just six year old beauty queens

Anyway you draw the short straw or chasing more headlines

This case sucks

Seems pretty straightforward to me he said some doped up Five Points citizen comes at a policewoman with a rock knocks her on her ass she defends herself with lethal and bob's your uncle he said not sure where the extenuating could be he said you'll be home by next week

Ah you know it's the simple cases that turn out to be the colonoscopies I said

What have you learned about the dead boy

Not much I said a philosophy grad student

Philosophy grad student huh no shit not my first guess he said he have a jacket

Shoplifting possession and a recent local jaywalking Boulder Police keeping the trains running on time

Traffic's not my gig he said anything else

I'm going to start with Shields I said see what she's about

Proof of your genius he said me I'd focus on the attacker maybe suicide by cop maybe just some bad Special K

Shields he said wouldn't call her squeaky but she's cool as a cuke not one to lose her head and start spraying you see my interview yet

No not yet

Check her out we all should be so ronin he said ice wouldn't melt in her *culo* Detective Fruscella pardon my French

Culo's Spanish I said thought I'd watch the tape I said

then have a sit down anything I should know beforehand Detective

Watch the tape he said no way it gets to the grand jury and no way she gets sued for some bullshit rights violation he said especially when the kid's tox comes back I tell you he said it all meets the eye

Thanks for your opinion Detective you do the nine yards weapon clothes confiscated Gun Shot Residue

I know you're Denver big he said but us hicks in the sticks still can do our jobs and besides he said the captain was breathing down my neck so hard I could smell what he had for breakfast last Tuesday so yeah Detective everything by the book

So nothing out there Detective

Not sure where you're going with this he said like I said seems pretty clear to me dude gets high causes trouble police respond dude attacks police police stands her ground end of story he said regrettable but understandable put yourself in her shoes he said what would you have done

Thank you Detective I'll have to watch the interview I said

OK I said I want us all to watch this and I want input I said impressions deductions intuitions inklings don't free associate but don't overthink either

Three oh four AM November twenty eighth two thousand and eleven Detectives Goldsmith and Sullivan present interviewing Officer Shields he said would you like a glass of water

No she said

So that's her he said

I've seen her around didn't know that was her she said

What's her height

Listed at five three

Five one if she's an inch I said

Swimmer's neck

Girlfriend swole

How big is Ratcliff I asked

Five seven

Officer Shields can you tell us in your own words what transpired the night of November twenty seventh

We were called for a possible trespassing and disturbing the peace violations at ten forty nine and responded immediately arriving at Arnett Hall at eleven oh two

Were you surprised to receive the call

No Detective why

Don't residence halls fall within the jurisdiction of campus police

Usually yes but we were told because of the football game and the holiday CUPD might be overextended so no we weren't surprised

She is cool he said

Looks Goldsmith right in the eyes takes her time answering

I still can't get over how cut she is he said

Easy there she said

What he said

We climbed the stairs to the common area and saw the suspect weaving around and laughing loudly we identified ourselves and asked for identification

How did he respond

He's not a suspect I said

He said he had a right to be there in the residence hall said he was a student and he was invited

Did he show you any identification

No

And then what

He became more agitated more belligerent she said started yelling and cursing

What did he say he said

Nonsense mostly she said he said fuck the police I remember

Anything else

I got as much motherfucking right to be here as any other motherfucker or words to that effect she said

Doesn't hesitate with the motherfuckers

Go on

As he's getting more and more belligerent confrontational we my partner and I she said determined that the suspect was becoming a danger to himself and others she said and so we decided he needed to be restrained and possibly removed

Did you discuss this with your partner

No we just gave each other a look

A look

We made eye contact we knew what it meant

Was there anyone else in the commons

No she said

Go on

As we approached the suspect he turned and ran down the far hallway we pursued but the suspect ran into one of the rooms and closed and locked the door

And then what happened he said

I followed him to the door and knocked on it identifying myself again she said

And Robbins

He followed

What then he said

We heard noises from behind the door inside the room

Noises

Stop right there I said is that a tattoo

Where

Left shoulder go back I said a little more there

Looks like it she said a butterfly

Can you zoom in

Definitely a butterfly she said

Not sure that's important I said go on

Raised voices arguing

And you did what

Continued to identify myself knock on the door and instruct the suspect to open the door

And when did Robbins decide to go fetch the janitor or custodian

A minute or two later we were worried about whoever else was in the room with the suspect and she said I think they're called RA's

And given that you'd seen Ratcliff and given your gender and size difference was there ever any thought given to

Robbins remaining with the suspect while you went to fetch the custodian

She didn't like that question

No she did not I said

Did she just give a little flex she said right deltoid

I can do my job Detective she said and I was nearer the door

I'm not trying to cast doubt on your ability to do your job Officer but given what transpired he said I am just wondering if there was any thought given that the physically smaller officer would leave to summon the custodian while the physically larger and more experienced officer would remain with the suspect and whatever situation the suspect was creating

RA she said

RA

No she said none at all

OK so Robbins left to find the RA and you continued to try to get Mr Ratcliff to open the door

That's right Detective

Go on Officer

She didn't like being put in her place

Can't blame her

I kept knocking and ID'ing myself and they kept arguing then the door opened inward and the suspect was standing in the doorway

She won't use his name she said

Was there anyone in the room behind him

I couldn't see she said

OK so what happened then

I backed up put my hand on my taser and told him to put his hands where I could see them

How did he respond

He moved toward me slow and big

Then what did you do

I backed up slowly we were too close and I thought maybe I could get him out into the common area and subdue him there use my taser if necessary the hallway was too narrow

So you backed up

Yes sir and then I noticed he's got this big rock in his right hand she said

You didn't see it before he said

No she said and just as I saw it he swung at me with it

He swung at you with the rock

Yes he lunged at me with the rock he wasn't fast but he lunged at me and his torso hit my knees and knocked me down

Did he swing or lunge at you

Swung definitely swung

What part of his torso hit your knees

I don't know she said I guess it was his shoulder

So you were on the ground on your back and he was where now

He was near my feet

And what was he doing

He was lifting himself on his knees he was going to come at me with that rock again

Was he saying anything

I don't remember no I don't think so she said

And what were you doing at this time

I was scrambling Detective backing up on my bum he hits me with that rock that won't be good she said he was a big man she said

Stop it I said

What are Ratcliff's measurements I said from the coroner

Let's see he's listed at five foot seven one hundred thirty five pounds he said

Five seven one thirty five is not a big man

They're both down and he came at her with that stone

And she's what I said

On her ass he said

No what's her height and weight again

Five three one twenty

More like five one one twenty

She's not overweight BMI probably like 18

BFP like 15

What the hell are you talking about I said

BMI Body Mass Index and BFP Body Fat Percentage she said

Means she's shredded he said

Big time she said in good shape

But Ratcliff is average height and skinny so what did she see I said

She saw the rock he said

He's only got fifteen pounds on her

She saw the rock he said

Go on I said

So you were scrambling backwards and he was pushing himself up to his knees what were you saying were you saying anything at this time

I was telling him to stop drop the stone put his hands on his head she said

And he wasn't responding

No she said

So you were scrambling and he rose up on his knees and now what did he make another move with the rock

No Detective I wasn't going to give him that opportunity

When did you pull your weapon when he was on his knees or before

He was beginning to raise himself to his knees to have another go at me with the weapon the rock he was carrying in his right hand

And he wasn't saying anything

Not that I recall

And when did you draw your weapon when he had reached the upright kneeling position or before

I drew it before he reached the full upright position and could attack me further again I didn't want to give him the opportunity to use physical force against me

So you drew your weapon as he was rising to his knees to attack you then what he said

I fired my weapon

How many times

Three times she said

And what did he do

He was hit and he fell forward

On his stomach he said

On his stomach she said

But if you fired and hit him why didn't he fall backwards either on his back or against the wall he said

He was on his knees and his body weight was still balanced forward

So he hadn't yet reached an upright position he said he was still on his knees he said

She looks pissed she said

He was rising up to hit me with the rock I fired before that happened she said

And your fired three times why not once or even twice

I wanted to stop him from attacking me she said and wasn't sure that two times would stop him she said

Why didn't you use your taser he said

Same reason she said I wanted to definitely stop him from attacking me with the rock

After you fired at him what did you do he said

I got up and ascertained that he was incapacitated then I turned my attention to the room behind him I kept my weapon drawn and stepped over him and proceeded down the hall in order to secure the room she said

Was the door opened or closed

Closed but not locked

What happened then

I opened the door and found the girl Frazier sitting on the bed weeping I did a quick sweep of the room keeping my weapon trained on her the bathroom door was open and I quickly ascertained that the room was empty save for me and the girl I then made sure Frazier was unarmed before I holstered she said

You zip tie her

No she said

Why not he said

She was upset Detective not hostile and she was unarmed I saw no reason to zip tie her

And then what

I went back to check on the wounded suspect but I saw that Robbins had returned I informed him the room was secure and he checked Ratcliff for vitals and called for an ambulance she said I called the precinct and reported the shooting I returned to the room and noticed what appeared to be hashish and smoking paraphernalia which I wrapped and packed she said Detectives Dworkin and Bergvall arrived a few minutes later she said and then you two arrived Detective when I surrendered my weapon

Why do you think it was hashish

I smelled it

Do you have anything to add to this Officer

No sir I do not she said

Take your time he said be sure

No nothing she said

Interview terminated at three thirty three AM November twenty eighth two thousand and eleven

Wish I could be that unflappable he said

Who called it in I said

A student Nancy Belhomme of Englewood called campus police who relayed it to us

How did she call it in I said

What do you mean

Was it nine one one or non emergency

Let me check he said it wasn't nine one one it was non emergency

Do we have a recording of the call

Nothing logged in

Call the campus police and ask for the recording I said any video

Not of the hallway we can see the suspect come in a couple of hours before

He's not a suspect

Sorry

He's dead

Sorry

Don't the dorms have security cameras

They usually do in the common areas but they decided to reboot and repair during Thanksgiving break figured everyone would be gone it's an old dorm and the system's less than robust so nada

And no bodycam

Next year Detective if the union agrees

So nothing to corroborate OK I'm going to go talk to her myself Carter I want you to suss out anything you can about her Springs' record she if she had any complaints if she ever fired her weapon or tased anyone Williams you get any info on the Black Existentialists

No not yet Detective

Well try the philosophy department again find out

which professors Ratcliff was working with see if we can interview one or more who identified the body

I don't see it in the file here it is a Ms Virginia Ratcliff mother

Find out where she is I said

There's no phone number listed he said

Ask Goldsmith I said or the Duty Officer and get me a recording of that initial call

Let me get my coat

GONE, GONE, GONE
BOULDER POLICE HEADQUARTERS

Occupy Occupy Fuck the Police Fuck the Police
Occupy Occupy Fuck the Police Fuck the Police

Justice for Ratcliff Justice for Ratcliff

Don't Shoot Don't Shoot

Justice for Ratcliff Justice for Ratcliff

Don't Shoot Don't Shoot

Cold I said and bright

Hooligans he said

Your Captain thinks that these hooligans must be from out of town although all I see is a bunch of trim young white people

I don't understand

Maybe Vail or Aspen maybe Ikea I said

Spoiled fucking brats

Everyone has troubles Sergeant I said even the young where's your car

Detective Fruscella Detective Fruscella

Yes

I'm Lieutenant Teare of the BPIO I'm sorry I wasn't here to greet you when you arrived she said but I had to dialogue with the media and then the university provost and lawyers she said the University of Colorado is extremely concerned about the matter she said extremely concerned

No doubt I said

They'll be making a statement at four this afternoon she said and best practices she said suggest your attendance

Why I said

Why she said well to indicate to the state and the country that CU deeply regrets the tragic incident and pledges its full support to BPD and the DA's Office to investigate fully the tragic incident and to offer its deepest condolences to the family of the victim

Tragic victim I said

Excuse me she said

Another bad idea in a case composed of such look I said I've never not once as in zero times found it useful to either involve or to become involved with external parties during a police investigation I said it makes no difference if these external parties to the police investigation are ostensibly internal to the said police investigation or unequivocally external to the said police investigation the fact is unless they are working directly on the case at hand they are by my definition external to the investigation no matter what organization they might be internal to it doesn't even matter how external these parties are to the investigation there's no prize I said for getting close external is external when I see external parties involved I said or attempting to become involved in investigations I said I see interference and by interference I mean attempts to influence the outcome of investigations which naturally I resist I said although resist is too weak of a word I said more like oppose or refuse that's the word I said refuse so when I see you I see an external party because as far as I can see you have nothing to add to the investigation I said no information no clue I said in short nothing that can be of any use to the investigation quite the opposite in fact I see you as nothing but a hinderance I said the opposite of useful an interfering hinderance I said so I'm not sure what conversation we could or really should have

I'm not sure I'm understanding you

Your interfering hinderance is made all the more egregious by your unthinking use of corporate language I said I agree that the modifier unthinking in this case is redundant I said as there is never an example of the use of this corporate language as being anywhere near to thinking I said and perhaps now is not the time to discuss how this corporate language has been allowed to spread like the virulent contagion it is I said to spread and infect every aspect of our lives especially I said the aspects of our lives which are spectacularly unsuited to the use of this unthinking inappropriate virulent corporate weasel speak aspects of our lives that in some cases like this particular case quite literally involve questions of life and death I said but in any case I said it's disturbing to see how this unthinking virulent corporate language has infected and sickened police work I said infected and sickened police thinking I said so you see Lieutenant Teare that as I said I see you as nothing but a interfering hinderance spreading an unthinking infecting and sickening virus I have little interest in cooperating with you

Occupy Occupy Fuck the Police Fuck the Police

Occupy Occupy Fuck the Police Fuck the Police

I onboarded Captain Christian completely regarding your responsibility for attendance

You may very well have Captain Christian's agreement however I am of course not Captain Christian and I have other reasons for refusing to cooperate for refusing to participate in your judicial academic Noh theater although maybe Kabuki is more accurate you all will be wearing makeup instead of masks because by participating I would give the illusion of subscribing to your unthinking corporate language use let me ask you this do you have children I said

No she said

No of course not I said but I do I have a son I will put this in the second person I said so that maybe just maybe you'll see what I mean let's say that you had a child and let's say he attended the University of Colorado actually I said let's not put this into second person the comprehension sympathy or empathy created by this rhetorical exercise will be eclipsed by the violence of what I am about to suggest a violence that should always remain in third person I said let's say a child another's child some child attends the University of Colorado as safe and lovely a place as you can imagine this child attends this sweet lovely idyllic university on the picturesque pristine old world style campus what could go wrong right I said but then one night one beautiful fall night after a football game this son somehow is gunned down by the local police on this now brutal bloody disaster of a campus this brutal bloody disaster of a campus where the glorious sunshine long legged students roman tiled roofs and sublime mountain landscapes serve now only to mercilessly mock the ashes of the dead to mercilessly ridicule the parents' grief and pain and so I said during some press conference or whatever you're calling this university ass covering I said some eurosuited piste tanned university lawyer gets up and says how sorry the university is that the police somehow fired a weapon and that your fine boy your beautiful fine boy your dutiful and loyal son somehow lost his life and that the university feels deep regret deep regret coupled with the staunchest determination to do and say everything to make sure that they comprehend what has happened and take all the necessary steps to guarantee that this never never never never never happens again and if need be make absolutely sure that if punishment is found to be appropriate then punishment will indeed be meted out justice above all will be served justice will be served and counseling made available then after the lawyer finishes explaining how very sorry they all are a woman police detective rises to her feet approaches the microphone and slowly and carefully with conviction and sincerity says exactly the same thing how the police very very very much regret this tragic incident and how they pledge to get to the bottom of this tragic incident with a thorough and transparent investigation and do whatever it may take to bring justice to this case how would anyone I said feel comforted reassured solaced by that

But you're from Denver a different police force entirely she said you're independent and non partisan

Justice for Ratcliff Justice for Ratcliff

Don't Shoot Don't Shoot

That distinction between police forces I said so vital

to you and I might be less crucial to the population at large I said for example I said with our current case under discussion do you think it matters I said to Ms Virginia Ratcliff I said mother of the deceased student killed by police I said at the University of Colorado where he attended as a graduate student I said do you think it matters at all that the police spokesperson hails from the Denver Police Department rather than the Boulder Police Department what difference do you think I said that could possibly make to someone burying their son I said I can't see that it would make the slightest bit of difference I said no I said in this case Ms Virginia Ratcliff will look up from her loss her total incomprehensible and terrible grief and see only the image of the university and the police standing side by side I said speaking bullshit first one then the other speaking only official virulent corporate language excretion that is even worse than the run of the mill virulent corporate language excretion because at least the run of the mill corporate language excretion what you speak every day what you *shed* I said every single day has a least no pretense to sincerity I said or if it does have pretense to sincerity it's a pretense everyone can recognize as pretense I said while this official specialized corporate language excretion today's bullshit carries with it the pretense of sincerity I said it's ass covering and job saving disguised as care for the dead and concern for his family I said so in sum I said there are three reasons or clusters of reasons I'm refusing to attend your press conference

Justice for Ratcliff Justice for Ratcliff

Don't Shoot Don't Shoot

It's not a press conference she said I wouldn't call it that

OK I said it's not a press conference or briefing public statement then there are three clusters of reasons I will not attend whatever it is you've asked me to attend I said I want to sum them up in case someone asks you why I'm not there first of all by attending the what should we call it briefing or statement if one can attend a statement I said the first reason I said is the fact that both the Information Office of the Boulder Police Department as well as whatever Public Relations Office and slash or legal council the university will be sending I said I consider external parties to the investigation and as such I said they are attempts to exert undue influence on the conclusion of this investigation the university I would argue I said has a strong interest in the investigation seeing how their brand could be damaged by an unfavorable investigative conclusion and so would try to avoid said unfavorable investigative conclusion by any or at least many legal means necessary I said and so I will I must avoid even the slightest appearance of impropriety by remaining separate from the university's presence and desires

Occupy Occupy Fuck the Police Fuck the Police

Occupy Occupy Fuck the Police Fuck the Police

The second reason I will be avoiding your press briefing or whatever you would like to call it I said is that I refuse to take part in the unthinking and vile contamination by egregious and virulent corporate language of A investigative police work B institutional accountability both academic

and governmental and C genuine regret sorrow slash grief
regarding the death of a young man on university premises
I said I can't see how one can avoid this contagion I said
this infection by an unthinking unalive algorithm injecting
semantic particles of pure stupidity and refusals to think
into living lexicons and replicating all the mindless
stupidity and absolute whitewashing of anything genuine
or thoughtful destroying the cells of police thinking from
within I said destroying the cells of academic freedom and
responsibility from within I said destroying the possibility
of true grief and regret from within I said destroying all
and any truth I said in other words pure bullshit last but
not least I said I don't want to intimidate or frighten the
Ratcliff family the remaining family of the deceased I said I
don't want them to believe that there's a united police front
or that there's a police front united with a university front
that would be a mistake to my mind any one of these three
reasons the external investigative influence reason the
virulent corporate language infection reason or the united
police university front reason would be sufficient I said to
keep me away but the presence of all three just add to my
resolution to avoid your press release conference briefing or
statement I said like the plague

Justice for Ratcliff Justice for Ratcliff

Don't Shoot Don't Shoot

It is what it is I guess Detective you understand that
the current chain of command necessitates that I inform
Captain Christian of your decision she said

Of course Teare

So we won't circle back on this but you and I will need
to have to tag up to discuss modes and methods of communication you know enough not to talk to anyone outside of
school without me present yes

Yes

And you do realize we need to get on the same page very
soon Detective she said we are on the same team after all

Is there anything else I said

No I'll be in touch she said let me make sure I have your
phone number ok good she said

I'm not good with those types I said those public relations
types those quick talking public relation mouths I said they
irritate me more and more I said whenever someone tries to
sell me something and those public relation mouths seem
to do nothing but try to sell me something I said it irritates
me more and more I said when I got up this morning I was
in a perfectly fine mood yeah I was in a perfectly fine mood
when I got up kissed my kid had a long cup of coffee smiled
on the way to the precinct I thought it would be a fine day
I said and I get to the office and the day quickly goes to shit
damn it I left my sunglasses in my car

You like it here Officer I said

I do Detective he said

What do you like about it I said

My girlfriend's a chef he said and this is a real foodie
town a ton of good restaurants good craft beers

That reminds me I said I haven't eaten lunch

Good hiking he said we like to hike take the dogs on
the trails

Oh yeah I said what kind of dogs

Golden retriever and a goldendoodle he said

What's a goldendoodle

Golden retriever and poodle mix

Fancy dogs I said

 Not really

I might have to get something to eat after the interview any recommendations

Depends on what kind of food you like Detective there's a vegan Mexican place that just opened by the station

My father in law's a non vegan Mexican don't think he'd let me back in the house

There's Thai and Indian close the Kitchen is excellent but crowded although they have communal tables Salt or Jax seafood do you like pizza Frasca the best food in Boulder has a pizza joint on the side that's great Napoletana good ingredients the Black Cat is open for lunch although he said they're kind of pricey they do a great farm to table thing for dinner

Speaking of which do you know where I'm staying I said

No he said I don't

I should have asked your Captain Christian it doesn't make sense for me to drive home then drive back early tomorrow I said he didn't mention anything to you

No he said nothing

I have a meeting with the District Attorney what's his name early this evening then we're going to go over the recordings and transcripts with a fine tooth tonight and then I want to talk to Ratcliff's mother and if possible one of his professors depending tomorrow and we still haven't read over the witness statements last thing I said I want to do is to drive back and forth to Denver I'll get a hotel I said but I assumed perhaps prematurely that you all would put me up I brought some clothes and things with me

I'll text Ms Fitzgerald she takes care of things like that

That would be great I said

Will do he said

So I said where does Officer Shields live I said

Northeast side of town off Gunbarrel

Nice hood

Kiddy condos and concrete he said retirees IBM drones we busted a prostitution ring there last year

First of all what are kiddy condos and second what prostitution ring

Kiddy condos he said are condos parents buy for their kids to go to school for four or five years then sell at a profit and yeah there was this white collar escort service for these IBM bros although they didn't escort anyone anywhere the women would simply drive over often on their bikes spend an hour then off to the next bro we busted ten girls and two madams we called it Operation Red Bull

Any girls underage

No

You bust any johns

No just warnings he said Captain's decision

Lovely I said

We didn't prosecute the ladies he said just deported them a few were from Haiti he said but most from eastern Europe

Who was the lead detective
Goldsmith he said
Of course I said of course

Officer Shields Officer Darcy Shields how do you do I'm Detective Fruscella and this is Sergeant Jones we'd like to ask you a few questions if you don't mind

From Denver right

Yes that's right may we come in

I didn't know when to expect you I was just about to go for my run can you come back this evening or tomorrow even

I'm afraid not

All right well come in I have to text my friends I run with a couple of girlfriends then we do SAC afterwards

SAC

Saturday Afternoon Club we have a resie at the Rio it's packed on Saturdays

Thank you we shouldn't be longer than an hour perhaps you can still make your Saturday Afternoon Club

Sorry about the mess I like to do resistance before cardio let's see maybe you can sit there

Sergeant Jones will set up his phone to record this conversation

What's this for again I already talked to Detective Goldsmith and I'm sure that was taped

As you know by now Officer this is routine I'm the lead detective not Goldsmith

I was attacked and in imminent danger of bodily harm you're not IA are you

No we're not Internal Affairs and I need to hear your story first hand

The union said I shouldn't talk to anybody without one of theirs present

There are two problems with that Officer Shields first of all if you call the union they'll send an attorney and we'll have to wait for said attorney maybe here maybe at the station it's Saturday after all and you'll likely miss your Saturday Afternoon Club at the Rio the second problem with contacting the union and involving an attorney is that the moment you involve an outside party we move across the table where before we were sitting next to one another the two of us looking at the case from the same angle now with an attorney present we're sitting on opposite sides looking at the case from opposite directions opposing one another so to speak I said and to be frank I said I can't see that as a good choice for you

So we're on the same side she said

Yes I said we're both trying to find and articulate the truth

I know what happened I was attacked under imminent threat of bodily harm as it says she said I defended myself Detective

Our audio and video are good Detective we're ready to roll

I don't know why we have to do this interrogation again

Interrogation is not the right word I said I don't think

What then conversation chat are we going to dialogue

Interlocution I said no that's not right either

That's a fancy word she said whatever you want to call it I don't understand why we have to do it again I was in imminent danger of bodily injury

Interview is nice and benign I said

I was attacked and I defended myself I have a right to defend myself

Do you like music Officer Shields

Is this part of the interrogation

Please answer I said do you like music

What kind of question is this Detective she said do I like music of course I like music do you always ask this question Detective and does anyone ever answer in the negative no I hate music can't stand any sort of tune

Do you like going to concerts

Yes I do she said but I am not getting the relevance of this Detective

But you do understand the difference between listening to a recording and seeing a performance in person it's very different you must agree I said being there in person sharing space and time with the musicians is extraordinarily richer and more complex than simply inserting a cd flipping a switch or two and listening at home

I have earbuds

The live performance works on many different levels and there is just so much more to experience I said you can see the performers and how they interact with their instruments as well as how they interact with each other

You could see me we were Interview Room Three there's video there

You can also hear nuances and slight distortions depending on the room the physical space as well as the crowd and the objects surrounding I said

It's more fun I agree but I still don't see the point she said

You can feel the bass in your feet sometimes your body your gut there are even smells and tastes if you're having a drink or with someone

Whatever she said I don't mean to be disrespectful Detective so maybe we could start

You asked why I had to question you again I thought I would answer I used to be a musician a pianist I said and I always liked to play the hard pieces the ones everyone said were too difficult when I was in middle school I wanted to play Beethoven's *Hammerklavier* for my seventh grade recital I said I loved the way Alfred Brendel played it and I really wanted to play like him there's this high A sharp after a trill in the Fugue near the end that's really hard to reach even with my big hands and Brendel does it really strong sweet but tremendously powerful and I could never figure out how he got up there from the lower octave C C sharp trill I said I tried a bunch of different fingerings but I could never understand how he hit it you're moving lower to hit the C and then have to change direction for the A sharp I could barely brush it with my pinky and if I tried to use my ring finger I'd be a fraction late I worked and worked on that I said played that measure hundreds of times I don't think I ever got it right but six or seven years later I said I had a masterclass in college with one of his students a Miss Ramp who said he kept his right hand going down to play the bass and crossed his left hand over his right for the A sharp like this it never occurred to me it was brilliant I said but there was no way of guessing this from just listening to the recording I said how he got from there to there

Still not sure what you're on about she said

I want to see how you get from C to A sharp I said I want to see your hands

My hands are right here

It's strange Officer Shields things have changed whereas before you were attempting to find the language that best aligned with your experience now you are trying to find the language that bests aligns with your previous language I said and my role as the listener viewer reader is to note the discrepancies between your two stories or rather the discrepancies between your two versions of the same story to note the differences between the two performances and to discover if these differences are significant if they in fact signal a difference not only between the two recounted versions but between the two recounted versions and what actually happened I said because that's really what we're after isn't it Officer Shields not the telling of what happened but what actually happened

OK she said if you want the same old same old

But it's not the same is it Officer Shields as I said I said this upcoming recounted version this recounted version yet to be can't help but be compared to the recounted version that was before whereas the first recounted version the recounted version that was had no previous recounted version to compare to the telling of the first recounted version has irrevocably changed all subsequent tellings just as this second telling will in fact irrevocably change the third telling and so forth we can't unsee or unhear any of the tellings can we Officer Shields

Who talks like this

And another thing Officer Shields an exact or nearly exact retelling is perhaps just as suspect as a retelling full of inaccuracies I said although neither suspect or inaccuracies are strictly speaking accurate suspect in this case implies an *a priori* suspicion which would indicate that I already have some idea that your telling does not align well enough with the transpired events I have no feeling yet about this which is to say that I have questions about how in fact your telling aligns with what actually happened but these questions are not answers and if I can have or do have no suspicions then the word inaccuracies is inaccurate as well for that would imply that I believe or suspect one of your versions more perfectly aligns with what happened than the other and as I've said I said I have no answers only questions about that but regardless an exact retelling by you I said one that aligns perfectly with your previous telling would imply memorization a focus on getting the right words together rather than a focus on finding the words that best align with what happened too many discrepancies mean you can't keep your story straight two few mean you have nothing but a memorized story

We got the call about ten fifty that night

Do you like jazz Officer Shields

Excuse me Detective

Jazz jazz music when you said you like music did that include jazz music

I don't know much about it

I don't particularly care for it myself I said I'm a classical girl through and through although I do like Prince my son laughs at that but mostly I prefer classical music my son likes jazz music plays jazz jazz piano he plays classical music too but he prefers jazz music there's a big difference you know

I guess she said

Obviously there are differences even if you don't know much about jazz music or classical music you can guess there are differences anyone who has heard in the most superficial and naïve manner a classical music piece and a jazz music piece would understand that there are innumerable differences between the two this is not to make any judgement as to which is better merely saying there are innumerable differences between the two is not to implicitly or explicitly rank the two in any way my son plays jazz music he wants to study jazz music composition which I find rather unusual I said but maybe unusual is too weak of a word I said maybe unusual doesn't adequately align with my feelings of distrust skepticism or suspicion even of jazz music composition do you know why I said

No idea

It's that word composition I said one of the more important differences between classical music and jazz music is the word composition composition for classical music most all of classical music even the modern or post classical music is the reliance on or use of the written score composing as writing or writing as composing when we think of classical composers Beethoven comes to mind but even the more modern classical composers like Schoenberg or Cage we think of writing sitting working the notes out at the piano and then writing the notes down and once finally the notes are written down tweaked once or twice then published then that musical score becomes the standard the ideal and every performance attempts to realize that ideal now there might be slight disagreements room as it were for interpretation I said to realize that ideal but this room for interpretation these slight disagreements are relatively minor I said often having to do with tempo accents and volume but never or usually never with the notes themselves with the notes that are written down so while Glenn Gould might hurry through the Goldberg compared to Angela Hewitt say they both play B natural as the first note of the Variation Number Two there is I said a platonic ideal of classical music a standard against which interpretations are often judged although it is true speaking of Glenn Gould and Goldberg that sometimes interpretations themselves can become standards let's leave that out for now I said anyway my point being that in classical music there is the written composition and that written composition is the standard by which every performance is judged more or less but in jazz music composition means something very different in jazz music composition and improvisation are not separate composition *is* improvisation and improvisation *is* composition I said does this make any sense to you

I don't know what you are talking about

In jazz music composition means something different this is from watching listening and talking to my son and I've always known men who were interested in jazz music that's probably why I never liked it could never stand the guys who were into it but in jazz music there are three maybe four compositional let's call them strategies jazz compositional strategies one can improvise with structure or method completely internalized and maybe eventually by improvising for enough time this internal structure or method becomes discernable to others I said maybe eventually sooner or later in time I said the internal patterning the internal jazz music structure becomes audible to others to jazz music listeners I said but you know who has that kind of time and although sometimes this improvising is recorded it is never I said or hardly ever written down so the question I have is this is this improvising in fact a compositional strategy at all in classical music terms I would answer no but in jazz music terms one would have to answer yes this is a valid jazz music compositional strategy there are jazz music compositional strategies I said more pertinent to our discussion one is to begin with chords or chord changes harmonies in time I said chord progressions and then devise or improvise a melody over these chord changes or one can go the other way start with a melody and then try to fit the chord changes to accompany it both are popular jazz music compositional strategies I said a soloist improvising a melody over pre existing chords and working things out or playing the melody first and then finding the chords working things out that way working things out by playing the chord progression and the improvisation over and over again or playing the melody and improvising the chord progression over and over again until the chord changes solidify and the chord improvisation is no longer improvisation or the melody solidifies and the melody is no longer improvisation I said by playing repeating what you've played before so that sooner or later the chord changes are repeated in the same way more or less and sooner or later the melody is repeated in the same way more or less sooner or later I said the improvisation becomes no longer improvisation and becomes more or less I said repetition maybe first the chord changes maybe first the melody maybe both at the same time but sooner or later the chord changes and the melody both become repetition not improvisation and then *voila* you have a jazz music tune sometime in that process the song is recorded and sometime in that process the song is written out and published but the thing is the thing that differentiates jazz music compositional strategies from classical music compositional strategies is that in jazz music compositional strategies neither the written nor the recorded is considered the standard to which all further repetitions must observe neither the written nor the recorded arrest the play of interpretation and improvisation I said rather both the written and recorded work to instigate or precipitate further improvisation and interpretation the written or recorded is not the platonic ideal not the last word I said rather the written or recorded is simply the initial comment the opening statement upon which the conversation proceeds and expands I said can you imagine Beethoven enjoying an interpretation of his Moonlight Sonata that changed the key to C major and sped the tempo of the *Adagio* to *vivaci* no I said not that he could hear anything anyway you can start with a chord progression and improvise a melody or you can start with a melody and improvise a chord progression but even though your improvisation may be recorded or written and even though both become less improvisation and more repetition I said the repetition never arrests the improvisation I said the composition then is both repetition and improvisation I said

When are you going to ask me what happened she said

In time I said in time I haven't talked about improvisation yet the thing about jazz music improvisation the thing I don't like is that with jazz music improvisation you never know where you're going to end up and not only do you never know where you're going to end up I said you also never know how you're going to get there with classical music performance on the other hand you always know where you're going to end up and you always know how you're going to get there for example I said I know that with a classical music performance say Goldberg that the *Aria* starts and ends with G in both hands and that the bass line in the final measure contains a passing quarter note D I like this knowledge I appreciate this knowledge but with jazz music improvisation jazz music improvisation that quickly becomes or rather always is jazz music composition there's never any certainty there is always the possibility

that you start with a different note than expected and end
with a different note than expected even with the more
rigid forms the twelve bar blues music form or the thirty
two bar jazz music form there's never the necessity or
even the desire to keep pitches tempo relations time key
accents chords everything or anything consistent one falls
into patterns of improvisation in jazz music improvisation
but these patterns may or may not be discarded may or
may not be repeated may or may not be modified from one
performance to another in jazz music improvisation it's
never a matter of knowing it's always a matter of wondering
and that constant openness and uncertainty bothers me
and what makes good jazz music improvisation as opposed
to mediocre or even bad jazz music improvisation if it's not
hitting the notes that should be hit that are already there
so to speak if it's not technique or rather if it's not only or
primarily technique I said so what is it what makes good
jazz music improvisation I said it's surprise I said or rather
it's the moment the exact moment when surprise becomes
inevitability that's what makes improvisation I said that's
what makes good jazz music as opposed to good classical
music which is the moment when expectation becomes
inevitability jazz music is built on surprise classical music
is built on expectation but where does improvisation come
from how does it happen how does one choose a dotted
quarter C followed by a D flat eighth then a B B sharp D
triplet what goes in to constructing that decision I said
what goes in to playing that figure on the fly as it were
I said and what is it that makes such a decision seem so

perfect so inevitable as if no other choice were possible practice you may answer I said but practice doesn't explain everything I said great technique does not always create great improvisation even I know this I said even I can hear this I think improvisation is the combination of three main areas of influence I said three main centers of gravity as it were I said the first is the player's past including all of his life including all of his playing and practicing including all of his entire being conscious subconscious and everything in between up until that point he plays the dotted quarter C I said everything he's heard everything he's played everything he's lived through everything he's experienced up to that dotted quarter C the second area that helps influence that decision is the people he's playing with let's say he's a horn player what's the drummer doing how's the bass player moving things along and how's the rhythm guitar handling the chords is he now using a first inversion instead of the second are they playing with the beat behind the beat slower than last night faster etc and the final influence to his decision is the audience how are they responding are they talking laughing listening intently and how might he best respond to the audience's mood and attention

What does this have to do she said with your questions to me

I am getting to that Officer Shields there's a final jazz music compositional strategy I need to elucidate I said and that's to improvise over previous music either harmony melody or both I said to take a previous tune well known or not jazz or not and to improvise with or against it play it straight or slant close or far align with the previous as best you can or twist it so that it's more or less unrecognizable or recognizable only to a few to take something familiar comforting known and then to improvise over with or against there's a lot to like here the best of both worlds to take the familiar and to make it new that's something I said this is a common jazz music compositional strategy I said and one that is very popular

Are we still talking about music

That's a very good question Officer Shields an excellent question I said let's come back to your case I said you experienced something significant and undeniable even traumatic and you were then asked to recount that experience to put that experience into words correct and so initially with Detective Goldsmith you were asked to improvise a telling a recounting of your experience you didn't rehearse your interview did you

Of course not

You didn't go over your story with anyone first did you with Robbins for example

I didn't talk to anyone

So in a sense you improvised your interview you took the questions from Goldsmith and answered them without much planning or forethought is that fair to say

I just answered the questions Detective Goldsmith asked she said

What strategy were you following Officer

I don't know what you're asking me

In your improvisation what jazz music compositional strategy were you following it wasn't just aligning with what went on in your head you had other players to consider there was Robbins sure but also Goldsmith and the woman who called it in your fellow officers and even the city itself so there was an external component to your song wouldn't you say Officer

I don't know what you're asking me a crime was being committed I responded and was attacked

My question is which jazz music compositional strategy did you use did you take a melody you had in your head and try to work chords from it or did you have the chords and try to work a melody I don't think it was either you didn't come up with something new Officer that was never your intention no you followed the last jazz music compositional strategy you took an old song a standard one well known to all and simply put your own spin on the song everyone knows

I was under imminent danger of bodily harm

Yes you keep saying that but it's the same old song wouldn't you agree the black man was where he didn't belong even though he was a student at the school he didn't belong there in the dormitory on a Friday even though he was invited even though he'd been there before he was big and threatening wasn't he his very presence was big and threatening

He was under the influence and belligerent did not follow police instructions we told him to stand down

The thing is your improvisation is neither surprising

He attacked me he procured a weapon and attacked me

Nor inevitable

I discharged my weapon to defend myself

We know how this is going to end I said we've always known how this is going to end

This is not fair to me she said I was doing my duty I have a right to defend myself

Yes I said so you've said so you keep repeating I said

Ok Officer I said let's take it from the top you got the call at what time I said

So Detective were her stories too similar or too different
   I'll have to watch the tape
She's more cut in person the woman looks strong
Then why was she so scared
Big high dude came at her with a rock can't really see the
mystery here
You would have done the same thing I said three shots
to the torso
I think pretty much all of us in that particular situation
would have done the same thing Detective maybe not three
shots but flat on my back a big strong kid coming at me with
that large ass piece of granite I definitely would have used
deadly to protect myself sure he said no doubt Detective
Everyone else feel like you do I said
No idea Detective no one's really talked about it but yeah
he said pretty much
As far as you can tell everyone's supports her hundred
per cent blue wall and all that
You say that like you think that's a bad thing
I think it's a bad thing a student an African American
student was shot and killed in a college dormitory by a
member of the Boulder Police Department yes yes I do I
said I think that's a very bad thing
   OK
But beyond that I don't know Jesus Christ I said I should
get off my high horse my blood sugar's in the subbasement
I have got to find something to eat Fitzgerald text you back

Let me check yes she did he said she says she hasn't
heard anything from Captain Christian suggests you book
a hotel and keep receipts

Red carpet treatment huh Christian not living up to his
name

He can be sensitive

You have any suggestions

About the Captain

No about where to stay

Swank or simple

You all are paying or will be

Downtown there's the Boulderado or the new place the
St Julien the football game was yesterday so one or the other
probably has a room

Do the police have a rate with either

I don't know Detective

Any preference

One's brand new one's old school the Boulderado has a
couple of bars with food

The Boulderado it is

Hi I got your text

Yeah I got the whole night off surprise surprise thought
we could do something

I'm working I said in Boulder

Until when

I have a case I probably won't be home for a while

Why are you working in Boulder that black student who
got shot oh dear I'm sorry

Yeah I said it sucks at least I got a nice hotel the
Boulderado

I love nice hotels she said

I could come up she said

I don't know what time I'll finish

Put my name on the room she said I'll see you when I see you some time tonight

Detective Fruscella please come in I'm Cecil Pearl the District Attorney

Mr Pearl

Sit down sit down please

Thank you

You weren't at the media relations meeting today Detective

No I was not

I assume you had your reasons but it's important I think he said that the university and the city proper show solidarity he said show the press and the public that we're all on the same page the town needs to support the gown and vice versa

I explained to that media liaison Teare why I didn't think my appearance was necessary or even useful to the investigation I said I wanted to get to work

Does your work include interrogating Captain Christian as to the reasons we requested you to lead up our Critical Incident Team he said and while I understand your independence is perhaps an important component to your investigative success to quote a rather horrid cliché there's no I in team Detective

I thought the reason I was brought in was that I'm not part of any team

Cioran says he said for you who no longer possess it freedom is everything for us who do it is merely an illusion

What are you trying to say I said

This is not an ordinary investigation Detective that must be obvious to you by now the shooter has been identified the weapon impounded method opportunity and motive all obvious and known everything's present black and white cut and dry the only task you have is to put it all together make sure the narrative coheres

And what narrative is that I said

That's the hundred dollar question he said

A hundred dollars in Boulder isn't much

To you there are two possible interpretations he said either the police officer Shields was justified in using deadly force to protect her life and safety or she was not now we both understand I'm sure that whichever interpretation you arrive at is merely that an interpretation

Which is what it always is

Which is what it always is yes but unlike the interpretations you construct on your home turf your Denver interpretations he said the interpretations here the Boulder interpretations will be merely advisory we have another investigation underway a parallel investigation a parallel Boulder investigation that may or may not share similarities to your interpretation

Internal Affairs

Yes he said Internal Affairs so I'll have your Boulder interpretation Internal Affair's Boulder interpretation and many other Boulder interpretations he said some implicit some explicit some ambient some immediate I'll take all of these Boulder interpretations and create a final complete narrative it's my job to piece together all of these provisional Boulder interpretations and find slash create a complete Boulder narrative that will restore our self image

The stories you tell yourselves

Exactly he said what it means to be Boulder a safe progressive inclusive community

It's just sometimes that the third adjective makes the first difficult

We are not Denver Detective he said nor do we wish to be

In fact I said you do everything you can to prevent it

The lifestyles of both can be fulfilling he said and lively why compare the two

Why use the word lifestyles

Let's return to the problem at hand shall we the oddity of our current situation is that most if not all of the significant facts of the case the bullet points if you will are indisputable and seemingly unassailable the young man was under the influence uncertain as to what and to what extent pending tox screening he was causing a disturbance according to civilian and police eye witnesses was uncooperative belligerent and eventually attacked a police officer with the intention to cause severe bodily harm according to the officer said officer responded with deadly force it seems at first glance that your interpretation options your range of viable narrative possibilities is rather curtailed if not altogether limited

We both know that first glances can be deceiving

Of course Detective we also know that sometimes what appears to be the most obvious turns out in fact to be true sometimes we overthink sometimes he said hideous covers do in fact enclose hideous books but it appears Detective from your posture and demeanor he said that you may harbor contrary suspicions that you may desire he said to complicate or at least qualify our cogent if not conclusive bullet points

Are we really discussing a typographical affectation

I love facts Detective bullet points create bullet proof narratives one would think he said one would hope he said that a police detective would share my affection for and insistence on the truth

I don't know enough yet about this case Mr Pearl I've only been here a couple of hours I've watched the interview Officer Shields did with Detective Goldsmith and I've interviewed Shields and her partner Robbins but right now I'm not even sure what the bullet points are I said let alone whether or not I can complicate them I haven't even been to the crime scene yet

I'm not sure I'd call it a crime scene

I will I said say however that truth is not limited to pithy phrases separated typographically or otherwise from surrounding contexts I'm not at all convinced that accuracy or agreement of statement and experience always or even usually depends upon laconic abridgement I'm not persuaded I said that statements laid out neatly and separately detached from one another are *de facto* true I said truth doesn't exist in a vacuum I said there's always a story always a narrative surrounding

I wonder what ground we share he said

Of course I said I have no way of knowing what the other Boulder narratives will narrate that's the way it should be I said we both know how narratives can influence one another contaminate one another so that sometimes a narrative an important and perhaps even central narrative perhaps even the true or at least the *truest* narrative is overwhelmed even obliterated by external foreign infecting dominating narratives I said and this can happen I said whenever there's a narrative in place before other subsequent narratives can be constructed I said I know that in my own narrative constructing I said that if I begin with a too strong initial narrative often subsequent narratives get infected and obliterated I said even if the initial too strong narrative turns out to be incomplete misleading or more or less mistaken I said even if subsequent narratives provide information that definitely alters or even contradicts the initial too strong narrative it is the too strong initial narrative that survives and dominates I said and it is the subsequent perhaps true narratives that are obliterated so it's important I said even critical that the initial narrative not be too strong

I must admit to you Detective that your discourse gives me pause not because I find it particularly convincing he said I do not but because it signifies to me that not only do we not share much in the way of grounding but that given the vast differences in the foundations of our narrative constructing it might be difficult to find any common communication or understanding

It is also true I said that sometimes the initial strong narrative is unspoken unarticulated unthought or even if we are to veer into the psychological unconscious these initial too strong perhaps unconscious narratives often prevent any subsequent narratives from taking hold

Perhaps he said the fundamental differences in our respective groundings are directly related to the differences in our respective goals perhaps it boils down to he said how comfortable each of us is with doubt I don't allow doubt to prevent prosecution he said beyond reasonable doubt is not necessarily certainty

What is beyond reasonable doubt I said and which of these three words beyond reasonable and doubt is the most important the word beyond metaphorizes the doubt places it into spatial terms as if reasonable doubt is a border that we must somehow travel pass or penetrate through in order to arrive at an elsewhere at a place or placement outside or far from the now spatialized doubt this is an exceedingly strange place external to both reason and doubt a place I said akin to faith I said although I'm not sure I want to go there and what about the modifier reasonable I said a re-markably meaningless word or rather I said a remarkably unreasonable word in that the use of said word is always circular the word presents no evidence gives no cause but simply insists on its own unexamined and unexaminable unassailable conclusions its own unexamined and unex-aminable unassailable presence a word that is pure context or rather a word that destroys or prohibits context be rea-sonable what can that imperative signify that imperative completely negates the process of gathering and weighing evidence of thinking through cause and effect the process we normally ascribe to the verb reason there is no reasoning in reasonable I said it's a word that refers only to itself and doubt I said what can we say of doubt if reasonable refers only to itself then doubt signifies every instance where there is a gap between language and experience every instance where there is a difference between one experience and another every instance where there is a space between bullet points I said which is to say every experience at all and so where are we when we are beyond doubt which is to say where are we when we are beyond everything I said

I don't think like you he said I can't think like you I would sit here he said if I thought like you I would sit here he said if I thought like you not moving barely breathing paralyzed by all I didn't know how can you possibly construct any narrative at all if all narrative constructing is *a priori* subject to contamination by previous or subsequent narratives and beyond a reasonable doubt to me it means exactly what it says I believe doubt is something that reasonable men reasonable persons can have and I believe other persons can present the facts narrated in such a way that such reasonable doubt is dispelled if you don't believe that he said it's hard for us to have a conversation

No doubt I said

In fact Detective I would argue that this doubt dispelling is our very job yours and mine he said for those who work with the law and or for those who love and respect her it's the very fundament of our profession he said to shine the light of transparency truth and reason upon the festering darkness of ignorance rumor and suspicion he said and in this case particularly he said where the facts are present known to all obvious and indisputable to all he said still ignorance rumor and suspicion have managed to create and advance a competing narrative a counter narrative a narrative of doubt you've seen the protestors he said suspicious ignorant rumor mongers it is vital he said imperative he said that this counter doubt narrative be countered

So you've already decided I said

No as I said he said I will carefully consider all the possible narratives but he said what I mean by possible narratives are narratives formed by facts and by formed by facts I mean confined or limited to reality I will not entertain he said narratives that warp or ignore the agreed upon reality and the truth is Detective he said that any doubt I have is directed at you I must confess that I harbor great doubt about your ability is not the right word I am altogether certain you possess the ability but perhaps temperament or disposition ideology even I have great doubt as to whether your epistemology will allow you to provide a possible narrative a narrative that is sufficiently reality based as to in fact add to the overall beyond a reasonable doubt Boulder narrative that I must finally construct he said you were speaking earlier of the strength of the initial narrative and the immutable inability of subsequent narratives to alter the initial narrative in this case that's not the case he said our initial narrative where you were the best person to head up our Critical Incident Team has definitely been modified and perhaps even what was the word you used obliterated by our subsequent conversations what I will need he said what I will need from you is a preliminary report a pre narrative as it were so that I may ascertain whether or not you in fact are the best person for the job of constructing a narrative both possible and reality based I will need this preliminary narrative on my desk as they say by Monday morning

I thought there was no I in team I said you are not shy of the first person

This is not about me Detective he said nor is it about you I prefer not to hide behind the passive he said which reminds me the Boulder narrative is a community narrative what happens he said after I gather all the possible Boulder narratives and determine the acceptable Boulder narrative

You have two options I said you can present the case to a grand jury to obtain an indictment or you can decline to prosecute

There's another possibility he said

I don't see it I said

Usually when I present to a grand jury I'm looking to indict correct

Grand juries are a District Attorney's best friend what is it ninety nine per cent indictment rate

But it is possible that I present a case to the grand jury that they decline to indict isn't that right

Possible but unlikely

Think of this Detective I can convene a grand jury of

twenty three Boulder citizens a true representative of the Boulder community and the final Boulder narrative would belong to them to the Boulder community the final acceptable Boulder narrative would come truly from the Boulder people the People's Republic of Boulder indeed

Manipulated by you to decline to indict

You look tired Detective would you like a bottle of water I have Fiji and coconut

I had a salty lunch

Oh where

The bar at the Boulderado I forget the name

Ground floor or downstairs

Ground floor

The Corner Bar it's nice you should try The Kitchen folks like Frasca or the Black Cat but I prefer The Kitchen Jax Fish House is tasty the cioppino is good but the raw bar is great pricey but fresh you like oysters

I haven't eaten oysters in a while

I grew up in Colorado Boulder born and bred but give me a dozen blue point oysters or crab legs with drawn butter over a Colorado rib eye or lamb chop any day of the week and sushi he said don't get me started on sushi what's that sushi restaurant right off the highway he said the one where you eat outside in a courtyard

Domo

That's it I like that place that and the Sushi Den I need an extra couple of miles on my run after a trip to the Den you're not vegetarian are you we have a great little place on the mall Thrive raw food makes you feel great pad thai with zucchini noodles is one good cracker not too expensive either

I've been to the Sushi Den twice I think

You have a Jax in Denver as well he said are you what is it called pescatarian

No I eat meat

Blackbelly's out on Arapaho they do that whole animal snout to tail thing I said I'm not a steak guy but their locally sourced Wagyu sirloin with chimichurri might change my mind listen to me I sound like a chamber of commerce brochure you have work to do he said

I have work to do I said

Monday morning in my inbox I want that preliminary report

PRAYER (OH DOCTOR JESUS)
BOULDERADO HOTEL

I'm usually the one who doesn't talk she said I can see
now how disconcerting it is

I don't have the words yet for this I said I'm still trying
to catch my breath

Never underestimate a girl with her toys she said

I've always been turned on by expertise I said but that
was ridiculous

Are you trying to suggest I've been around she said

Oh no I said it's just that well let's just say I've never
experienced such dexterity especially from one so much
younger than me

I'm not as young as you think have you ever been
experienced well I have she said

Hendrix I said what do you know from Hendrix he was
way before your time

So

Before my time too to tell you the truth

Music's music no matter when it was made she said

Maybe I said maybe not

Are you one of those music snobs she said one of those
hipsters at the bar who get all bent out of shape if you've
heard of their favorite indy obscurity

No one has ever ever called me a hipster before

You are though a hipster music snob you're probably a
movie snob too or should I say film snob

Cinema I said cinema snob

Franny the hipster Franny the hipster

I don't mind being called a hipster nearly as much as I mind being called Franny

Franny the hipster Franny the hipster

I'm serious I said I'll arrest you

Arrest me huh she said put me in handcuffs

No one has called me Franny since my mother when I was like five it sounds like an old lady's name I said

About those handcuffs she said

You watch too much TV I said

I've never slept with the police before thought I'd go all in

I don't carry handcuffs anymore I said just the twist ties

I'm dangerous Officer she said you'd better tie me up now

Detective I said not Officer and I think the twist ties kind of hurt but to be honest I haven't restrained anyone in six or seven years it's usually a uniform who restrains I said while I read the Miranda you have the right to remain silent

My hands are dangerous weapons they can do this

I kind of like that

Or this

Mmmm I said I really like that I said dangerous weapons indeed what is that what are you doing

A new weapon she said you like

I'm not sure it's a little

A little what

A little intense can you turn it down or something

Sure thing how's that

Much better I said oh my

That's my rabbit she said and rabbits are a girl's best friend

I like the way it goes deep and works up there as well

Simultaneous vaginal and clitoral stimulation she said can't be beat

Accurate I suppose but rather clinical

They used to be dick shaped the new ones are more abstract I like these better dicks are so last century

My God this is embarrassing I said

Embarrassing why embarrassing she said

My body is out of control

Why is that embarrassing

I feel like some naïve thirteen year old discovering horseback riding

Like a virgin touched for the very first time

Oh jeeze slow down please I said Jesus slow down I said

Mmmm

Madonna Hendrix hmmm

The juke box at the bar

Dear God I said that was amazing is there something I can do for you I said

Not now she said just lie here and relax

Look at my pillowcase my eyeliner ran

I see

I did my eyes before you came I must look like a racoon

You look nice in this light

I'm not sure what to do my stomach muscles are a little sore I feel so languid

Excellent word languid nothing like a good fuck to help nail you to the universe you do know women get hornier as we get older true science

Do you have any tissue

Relax she said lie back

Are you sure there's nothing I can do for you

Just talk to me she said I like the way you talk she said

What do you mean how do I talk

Like you care she said that's not very well put most of the lesbians I've been with they talk and talk processing constantly the cis men well either they try to impress with abstract concepts and name dropping or else they don't say anything at all the bi women can be pretty good conversationalists but the bi women I've run into are all either just getting over someone or just getting into someone and so that's usually what we end up talking about I lose interest rather quickly she said I know very few bi men maybe that's my fault she said

And where would I fit in the aged and disastrously inexperienced I said

Oh *pobrecita* she said dry your tears the way you use language is incredibly sexy that and your huge hands I'd much rather hear about how you became a music hipster she said than your sexual insecurities

I am not a music hipster I was born a detective

That I don't believe she said

So what was I then a bearded lady

Parts model

Ha ha

Seriously you have exquisite hands she said huge hands for your wrists she said almost as if they were rendered by a near sighted sculptor

Thanks

You have excellent posture too she said that's the first thing I noticed about you that and you're not very graceful

What

You have a dancer's posture straight back but you don't move like a dancer you hesitate you seem unaware of your body in relation to other bodies or other objects in space it's like you haven't quite adjusted to Earth's gravity plus your calves are kind of undeveloped so even though you're snobby enough to be a dancer you're not she said

Why are you so convinced I'm a snob I said

The way your eyes constantly narrow and the fact that your lip is permanently curled she said so let's see not a dancer and probably not an athlete either she said not with that posture too upright for running and too short for basketball or volleyball and you don't really strike me as the softball type see what I did there

So you think I'm a bitch I said with judging eyes and a perpetual sneer

First of all I don't think you're a bitch and secondly she said there are far worse things to be than a bitch a fool for example or a chump and you're definitely no chump or fool she said and you don't dress well enough to be connected to fashion

Everyone thinks I'm a bitch I said including at least two police captains and three or four Boulder police probably

a coroner maybe even a district attorney and that's just
currently wait a minute what do you mean I don't dress
well enough to be in fashion I have some nice clothes some
things that look quite good on me

I'm sure you do she said and I haven't seen you really
tarted up yet she said you're too busy catching bad guys to
put all that thinking into how you're styling I mean who's
going to see you lowlife killers and paunchy fellow cops
I get it comfortable shoes a nice top and if you're feeling
frisky a pencil skirt above the knee she said enough money
to not be totally clueless but not enough time to give that
much of a fuck me I'm good with the punk ho look she said
sometimes a little more punk sometimes a little more ho
but the only people I have to impress are various classes of
drunks from pediatric oncology scrubs to homeless meth
heads impress them to keep their hands off my ass and a
few quid in the tip jar not to mention she said I'm blessed
with height

So I'm a short clumsy snob with good posture and big
hands

Military would explain the deportment she said and
maybe the detection obsession but you have a major
problem with authority I can't see you taking orders for
very long and I don't know much about soldiers but you
seem more cultured than the average jar head more brains
than brawn and besides she said did I mention you really
hate authority

No I was never in the military I said

So let's see very well spoken big hands good posture

hates authority middle class music snob went to no graduated from college widowed mother of teenage son

Of a certain age

Of a certain age prone to mild to middling self-pity
doesn't suffer fools what am I missing she said

The big picture

God is in the details she said like this

Mmm I said I thought it was the devil that feels very
very nice what is this

My little bullet she said sometimes I put this in at work
she said while I mix drinks it has a remote control

Oh oh my God I said that feels nice to me it's obvious
I said I'm cultured in quotation marks big hands straight
posture and a music snob I said it all adds up clearly I said
I want to kiss you so please please

Keep talking she said

I'll try I said I'll try oh dear anyway it's obvious to me
music snob straight back big hands wait for it ta da I studied
piano performance that's what I was before I became a
detective dear God dear Jesus I said what are you doing to
me

Keep talking

I can't right now I said

Keep talking

I can't right now

Keep talking

Whew

Mmmm

What about you were you always a sex worker

Ha ha no I went to college back east photography she said I don't think I could be a sex worker she said move your leg up a little

Like that I said

No more like that put your fingers here there see like that

I'd like to see some of your photographs

Slow down she said I could never be a sex worker I've no problems with it morally but aesthetically I definitely have aesthetic problem she said besides I'm too selfish

I get the aesthetic problems I said there's always some little thing that suggests it won't be worth the effort

Like a piece of lettuce in the teeth she said

Cheap shoes

That *sportlich* look she said

That must limit your Colorado partner pool

Thighs that touch sweatpants will never touch mine

What do you mean selfish I said

Fucking is often selfish she said we do what we do to get off good nothing's wrong with that

No nothing's wrong with that

It's like exercise she said like exercise from the gods

Ha ha

That's why monogamy jealousy makes no sense she said or if it does make sense it's usually a sense for the wrong reasons

I don't know I said

But the better you get off the better I get off too I very much like participation I very much like being taught new tricks she said

I'm the old dog

Giving pleasure can be the greatest pleasure she said

The greatest power too I said

But sometimes sometimes she said fucking is more than exercise

Hopefully I said

Sometimes fucking is a way maybe the best way maybe the only way of breaking through

Breaking through what I said

I'm not sure breaking through the walls of flesh and bone and skin breaking through to really touch something of the other person like what I'm doing now she said gently stroking your upper thigh my skin touching yours but also somehow trying to connect beneath the skin beneath this outer layer somehow if just for an instant connect touch experience something something more real yet non corporeal something present yet weightless and ethereal I think sex can do that sometimes allow access no matter how fleeting to some spirit beneath our skin

Hmmm

If only to be reassured for that instant that we're not alone she said

I don't feel I have much in common with other women most of the time

If only to be reassured for an instant that this isn't all illusion she said

Nor men for that matter

Sometimes I feel like I'm a different person from day to day she said or from afternoon to evening anyway I wasn't kidding she said I think fucking is a great way to nail you to the universe to open up somehow to open up to disintegrate and to feel for just a moment without the boundaries and borders of skin and meat to feel yes she said that I belong

Hmmm I said

But I only get this glimpse of something beyond the body when I surrender to the body she said

Hmmm

Sometimes I feel like I'm suspended in the air

Hmmm I said

I'm not making any sense she said and you don't suffer fools she said

No it's quite nice what you're saying I'm not sure I understand completely though

I don't speak as well as you that's what sex is for communicating with the different want to try something new she said

This is all new to me

I got a new toy yesterday she said and I haven't tried it out yet

Nice color pink what is it

It's called a Sona it's supposed to stimulate with sonic waves

What

Sonic waves directly onto your clit she said

Like music I said

Or voices she said

Kiss me first I said

I dated this singer once she said this guy with a beautiful

deep voice I always wanted him to sing while he fucked me to see if I could feel his voice through his dick that's not unreasonable right I mean his voice always made me wet I just wanted to feel it in my cunt instead of my ears she said

And

He never would do it she said we didn't last she said here let me turn this on

That's loud I said

Let me try over here she said you might have to hold it yourself

I don't feel anything

How about there

Just a little tickle

There

Yes I said

Yes

FISHERMAN, STRAWBERRY AND DEVIL CRAB
ARNETT HALL
UNIVERSITY OF COLORADO AT BOULDER &
NEWLANDS BOULDER CO

This is the stairway the officers took yes there are cameras above the door on each floor

Their whole system was being rebooted so nothing from inside we do have some footage from the outside the entrance

So they're walking up the stairs and they come to this door no window or anything they really can't see what's on the other side

No they just know what dispatch has relayed he said

And what's that again

Let me find it here an intruder is acting belligerent on the third floor commons of Arnett Hall do you feel threatened ma'am yes no I don't know you should go inside your room ma'am and close and lock the door officers will be there shortly stay on the line please

Belligerent's not a very definite word is it I said

I know what it means Detective

Ratcliff could have just gotten annoyed at being asked who he was and what he was doing there maybe said something we should talk to the caller what was her name

Nancy Belhomme

She's not still staying here is she I'd like to talk to her

I don't know where she is Lieutenant Teare is the liaison with the university

Does the transcript have a room number for her

No but we can ask the Lieutenant

You call she doesn't like me so they open the door and see what

During the interview Shields said he was weaving around and laughing loudly

That can be belligerent

Ok so we step in he's weaving around and laughing loudly now we identify ourselves and ask for his identification does his mood turn now was he giggling before and now that the cops are here shit gets real

He insists he was invited and he was a student

Is he still laughing probably not so he doesn't offer up any identification and things begin to turn what's the transcript say I said

He became more and more agitated belligerent

There's that word again

Yelling and cursing fuck the police and I'm a student I got as much motherfucking right to be here as any other motherfucker

And no one else is around not the woman who called it in not the girlfriend

No he said

So they ask him for identification he gets bent and starts yelling fuck the police now what

He goes from belligerent to confrontational

Oh so now he begins to focus his ire on the police I said

And they determine that he's becoming a danger to himself and others

What others no one else is here this is where they give that look to each other right

Yeah they make eye contact and decide to restrain and remove

Where are their hands during all this

I don't know

Do they have their hands on their tasers

I don't know he said

On their zip ties

No mention

Their belts

Don't know

Ok so they move in to try to restrain him and he takes off where which hallway

Probably that one with the tape

Yes so he makes a beeline for the room and the officers stumble through chairs and tables this place isn't very big I said and this is a narrow hallway so he runs down here and slams the door watch your head on that tape and they follow now what

They bang on the door and order him to open the door he said

And they hear what on the other side

Noises and then raised voices

Noises and raised voices then Robbins leaves right

Right

Makes sense there's not much room to maneuver I said ok so I'm banging on the door identifying myself ordering him to open up and Robbins leaves then what

The door opens inward and there Ratcliff stands

The door's locked you stand as close as you can I'll be Shields I'm knocking the door opens inward and there you are so I back up right

Yes she does puts her hand on her taser now she's backing up while he slowly advances

He advances and she backs up until what he swings can you swing there's hardly any room

Wait a little further see the marks

Ok right about here

First she says he lunges then swings

How do you lunge then swing

Like this

There's no room to swing unless you do it from your waist like an uppercut or downswing now what

He swings and misses and then knocks her down with his shoulder to her knees

His shoulder hits her knees and she falls backward can you do this try to swing at me then fall so your shoulder hits my knees can you do that

Not readily

Try again

When you swing you turn your shoulder that's natural it's not easy to do as she described possible but not easy if you hit me in the knees wouldn't I fall forward

Not if you're backing up

Hmm I'm backing up you lunge at me hit me in the knees and I fall backward is that possible then what happens

I'm on my stomach

Where's the bookend

Still in my hand

You didn't drop it

She doesn't mention him dropping it

He's lunging and falling hits her with his shoulder on the knees knocks her backward breaks his fall with his hands I assume and is still holding on to that bookend

That's what she said

I'm a little skeptical the choreography seems clumsy

He could have dropped the rock and then picked it up again

Unlikely

It seems plausible to me

Possible possible so you're on your stomach and I'm on my back here would you say he would have to be closer if she's feeling immediately threatened

Not necessarily

There were no powder burns on the clothes or skin

No

With her Glock 19 that would suggest at least three feet

Yes but when he gets up he has to move backwards see

Right he moves his torso back he physically can't move it forward while he's rising up he has to move backwards

He could rise up a bit then move his knees up under him like this

Possible but awkward she's clear back here and he's here I don't see how he's a threat now

You weren't there

I think she shot him when he was moving away from her you can get up now

It very well could have happened the way she and Robbins both described it

But Robbins wasn't present during all this falling and shooting I think Ratcliff came out of the room and maybe tripped or something I don't think he swiped at her with a large stone bookend I think he tripped knocked her down and then as he was trying to get up she shot him

She was threatened

She was frightened

She was assaulted

He tripped or maybe she just fell backward on her ass

He attacked her with that big rock that bookend look at the crime scene photos see there he's holding it tight in his hand

I'm not convinced about that what's the girlfriend's name

Frazier Serena Frazier

We have another address she's not staying here

Teare might

I'm supposed to meet the Ratcliff family in an hour and a half I'd like to speak with Frazier quickly beforehand see if you can get Frazier's whereabouts from Teare we can come back here if need be after I said

Thank you for seeing us Ms Frazier on such short notice I know this is extremely difficult for you and we promise not to take up too much of your time

I'm going to go to the memorial tonight and then my mom's coming tomorrow I just want to go home

Where is home

Oak Park outside of Chicago

I might try to interview you again later today I'd like to get to know Johan much better but for now we just have a few questions and then we'll be going I've read over the statement you've already given and I just would like to clarify a few things first of all let me make sure of this you and Johan were a couple yes

He called himself Joe not Johan

But you were a couple

Yes we were

An exclusive couple what I mean is that did either of you see other people

No we were together a traditional couple

For how long when did you start

We started going out about a year ago September

How did you meet

He was my sister's philosophy TA and I walked her to class one day and there he was my sister had said he was cute so I wasn't surprised he texted me a couple of days later and we went to dinner and then started going out

Did he usually spend the night in your dorm

No that was the first time

Why you'd been going out for over a year and this was the first time he spent the night at your place

No no this is my first semester in the dorm I used to live off campus we would often sleep at my apartment

But this is the first time he was going to sleep in the dorm why

He hated dorms made him claustrophobic he said

Was it only claustrophobia was there any other reason

What do you mean she said

I'm sorry to have to ask this but I'm trying to get a read on Johan's Joe's state of mind that night when you were together did you ever feel any agita or hostility from anyone on campus

Not really people were usually pretty OK with it sometimes we'd get kind of a surprised look Boulder doesn't have many black people or we'd get what we used to call the understanding glance of harmony and encouragement but usually there were no microaggressions or anything people didn't pay that much attention to us I don't think

So his friends were cool your friends were cool no tension that you could see

I mean not usually like I said there were surprised looks sometimes but no no one would yell at us or anything

What's your major Ms Frazier

I'm an MA student in sociology

Sociology huh so you'd notice if people were disapproving or rude to you as a couple

I'd definitely notice Detective

Was there any time that you felt either mild disapproval or something more serious

In Boulder

On campus

Maybe one or two times at this Philosophy Department party once one older guy a professor I think was hitting on me and then Joe walked up and you know put his arm around me or something and the guy made a face like what a waste and then I thought he was going to say something but he didn't

And when was that

That was at the Christmas party last year so late November

But nothing more recent last couple of days or weeks

No nothing

So you didn't notice any other what did you call them microaggressions or racist incidents the past few days

No nothing

Or weeks I said

No she said

So tell me about Friday night

We met downstairs at about six he had his recitation until four then he said he was going to go home and change maybe take a nap and I was working on a paper I worked through fall break had a ton of writing to do so I met him downstairs at six and then we walked to the hill for some food

Where did you eat

We got slices at Abo's

Then what

Then we went to the Secret Bar for drinks

What mood was Joe in

He was talkative happy

And no one bumped into you said anything gave you a funny look

No Detective

So what did you do at the bar what time did you get there

A little before seven it's close to Abo's we got there and met some of my friends Ally and Iliza and had drinks

That's Alexandra Gonzalez and Elisabeth Appiah yes

That's right we met them and sat at a booth and had drinks

How many drinks

I think we both had two drinks I'm sure I did Joe might have had three but I doubt it

How long did you stay

Until almost nine

Two drinks two hours

We're not heavy drinkers Detective Ally and Iliza probably had more

Did Joe get along with Ally and Iliza

Yeah I think so they're my friends but we'd all gone out before and he didn't say anything when we made plans

But no one fought and no one said anything to ruin the mood

No Detective we left on a happy note

Why did you leave

I don't know we just thought we'd go back to my room

What were your plans

You know Detective

No I don't

We wanted to get high and have sex Ally and Iliza stayed at the bar

Was Joe a heavy drug user

No he was not

Did you ever see him do any drugs besides hash or marijuana

No Detective

Shrooms hallucinogens pills coke meth
No Detective never not that I know
How often did he use marijuana
I don't know we used to get high once in awhile
Every night
No not every night
Every other night
No once or twice a week
During the day
Not usually maybe on a Saturday
Every Saturday
No once or twice we're graduate students Detective we can't afford to get high all the time
So then what
We walked back to the dorm
And how was Joe
He was fine a little tired maybe but still good
So you got back to the dorm when
About nine fifteen
Then what
We went in through the side entrance not the front then we walked up the stairs to my room and smoked some hash
And then
And then we had sex
And he was still in a good mood all through this
Yes he was
The hashish didn't change him the sex didn't change him
No he was happy relaxed

After sex did you notice what time it was

No Detective I did not

Then what

We smoked some more hash and he said he was going to go out into the commons for a while get some air she said

Was that normal

It was Detective he often got a little restless after sex he'd often wander around

So he wasn't angry or irritated or anything you could see

No

So then what I said

He got dressed and left I went to the bathroom then got back in bed I heard this commotion but I thought it was outside from the football game then I heard him yelling and so I turned on the light and got up and Joe ran in and locked the door

Go on

He was agitated freaked out saying they were always after him and he was just so sick of having to walk on eggshells around every motherfucker in the entire motherfucking world and I heard the police pounding on the door

Did they identify themselves as police

Yeah they did this is the police open the door this is the police open the door

How was Joe acting

He was getting louder and louder he was shouting leave me the fuck alone leave me the fuck alone

What were you doing at this time

I was trying to calm him down

Go on

Then he told me to get into the bathroom

What

Yes he told me to go into the bathroom he said he was going to go out there peaceful but that he wanted me out of the way out of the line of fire

Did he say line of fire

Yes

What did you say to that

I told him no fucking way but he told me he wasn't going anywhere until I got in the bathroom so I said OK

And

And I went I closed the door sat on the toilet seat heard the room door open and close then I heard the cop bitch screaming at him then I heard the shots

How many shots

Three

Then

I didn't move Detective I couldn't move I knew he'd been shot but I couldn't move I wished I'd brought my phone in with me

But you did leave the bathroom

I heard the front door open and then close and then I was able to get up and go to the bed to sit

Wait you heard the door open while you were in the bathroom are you sure

Pretty sure Detective

The front door opened and closed and then you got up left the bathroom and sat on the bed

That's right

Were you afraid I said

I was afraid of what I'd see I knew what had happened

And then the police officer came in

Yes and I started crying

Did she say anything

No she just looked around with her gun out

Did you see the other officer

No from where I was sitting I couldn't see out the door
she said

This is important did you ever see Joe with your bookend
in his hand

No I told the other policeman he must have taken it after
he sent me to the bathroom

But you didn't see him take it

No

Where was it

On my bookshelf

Which is where

It was right near the door to the left

So he could have grabbed it just before he opened the
door

Yes

But you didn't see him do that

No

And you're sure you heard the door open and close while
you were in the bathroom

I'm not sure but I think I did

What percentage sure

Eighty per cent sure

Thank you Ms Frazier you've been most helpful

What was that with door opening and closing

Shields I think she opened the door when Frazier was in the bathroom I want to take a look at that bookend was it dusted

What are you implying

There are a couple of things that don't make sense and some time that's not accounted for

I don't see it

My Man's Gone Now
Boulderado Hotel

Thank you for seeing me Ms Ratcliff I know this can't be easy for you

We've answered many questions from the police Detective

Fruscella I'll try not to take too much of your time Ms Ratcliff

I'm not sure what else we can add Detective and forgive me but I'm not feeling very loquacious since your police officer killed my son

It wasn't my police officer ma'am I'm from the Denver Police Department the Boulder District Attorney asked me to come in and oversee the investigation into the shooting of your child

I am sorry Detective she said but I can't see how this will fail to be a complete waste of time

Please Ms Ratcliff I said I just have a few questions please don't make me talk to this closed door thank you I know so very little about your son I said and I think it's important to understand something about what has been destroyed to understand something of what has been taken from us that's all I want from you Ms Ratcliff that's all I need from you I said

My son is dead she said there's nothing more to know

Come in she said

Who is the singer

Excuse me

The music who is the singer

Sassy she said Sarah Vaughn Sassy she said is helping me through this this hell

I'd like you to know Ms Ratcliff how very sorry I am

You want me to accept your condolences I don't

I have a son and I don't know how I'd react

No you can't know it's not the same the police don't kill white kids would you like some tea room service just brought it up

Thank you

Sit down I'll turn the music off

It's fine it's nice

They have a quite an assortment here Earl Grey Lemon Zinger Vanilla Rooibos Green Green Decaffeinated SleepyTime English Breakfast

Earl Grey would be lovely

My husband took our daughters to the protest with the white kids in front of the police station they're fifteen and sixteen he's never again going to let them out of his sight milk sugar

Just milk thank you

Hard to imagine what it is like she said to have your child murdered and your heart broken absolutely and then hours later to sit in a fancy hotel room having tea with someone who helped murder your son

I wasn't there I don't what to say

I'm neither ignorant nor blinded by grief to suggest that you were there in person Detective you don't all look alike to me she said I know you were probably miles away in another city maybe even with your son she said watching TV getting ready for bed but you were there in that dormitory hallway just the same if not pulling the trigger then loading the gun if not loading the gun then phoning to report someone who surely didn't belong you were there Detective and not just because you're a police either although that doesn't help no that doesn't help at all she said you were there

I don't know what to say I said I wasn't there

That is the one thing I cannot talk to the one thing we have got to get out of the way before we can have any conversation before we can even see each other as two people two women two mothers that one thing is your delusional exculpating ahistorical willfully blind God damned sense of innocence and by God damned I mean that literally she said

I don't know what to say I wasn't there

But why are you here she said why are you here now why are you here now in this hotel room worrying a grief stricken mother you know what happened or you know your version of what happened black man obviously where he doesn't belong acting loud acting uppity call the police black man refusing to listen refusing to obey draw my weapon black man threatening then attacking bang bang bang black man dying black man dying again what the hell are you doing here

I'm trying to piece together a picture of what happened that night Ms Ratcliff I said and to do so I need a better picture of your son I know this must come as a terrible shock

Shock she said shock I've not suffered any shock that's the tremendous and terrific pain of it don't you see that's what sticks deep down in the bottom of my gut the fact she said that this useless obscene premature degrading act of absolute violence is anything but a shock don't you see she said we always knew this could happen this knowledge this possibility preceded my son's very existence she said we understood before he was even born she said that there was the very real possibility that our son would die violently before his time at the hands of this country you can't possibly imagine that she said you can't possibly imagine what it's like to have that story that ending that fear to be present with you and your son for as long as he's alive like a caul or scar a mark of fate it's not she said a shock at all it's not she said unimaginable for me it's not she said unspeakable for me I have the language I've always had the language she said we've always had the language she said that's another of your gifts she said you've given us the language and the narrative of absolute terror the language the narrative of our children's destruction

I can barely hear your whispering

You can't imagine what it's like to know the story she said to know the ending but to go on with it anyway to think maybe it will be different this time maybe we can do something to change the conclusion we understood that we had to take great care right from the beginning we understood that we had to warn him train him drill him make sure he understood how to behave what to do what not to do and always always even if he was sure to defer she said right from the beginning we also understood we had to do more we had to control the environment as best we could we gave him a vaguely European name moved to Vail she said where we weren't a threat we sent him to Bennington where white people weren't so afraid and then grad school in Boulder where the police don't shoot he was a doctoral student in philosophy Detective at the University of Colorado in Boulder it was the safest place we could think of she said other than the moon we thought he'd be safe here he thought he'd be safe here but no Detective she said even in the twenty first century some of us still cannot escape our fate she said some of us still cannot escape the story you continue to tell of us so you see Detective it's not only the pain of losing a son but it's also the pain of fulfilling a pre arranged ending of completing a story told by others by calling it a tragedy the narrators can author a story that serves to edify and excuse these very narrators and convince that they have emotions and are therefore living sentient beings and that ultimately and practically they are distant and separate from the causes of said tragedy that's why you're here isn't it you want to fill in his character you want to find some flaw some glitch that in some way shows he deserved to be shot don't you suspect Detective more or less that in some small way my son deserved his fate maybe he shouldn't have been smoking dope maybe he shouldn't have been dating a white woman or at least not sleeping over in her dorm maybe he should have what stuck with his crowd stayed home something and even if you believe Detective that this was just bad rotten luck isn't there a part of you Detective a part of you that perhaps you're not proud of but a part of you nonetheless that believes that there was something about my son something in his character something maybe small and insignificant she said something maybe small and insignificant but something all too real that if it didn't invite it allowed allowed bad rotten luck to attach itself to my son allowed bad rotten luck to accompany him to the dorm that night allowed bad rotten luck to sass the wrong police officer and allowed my son's body to stop those three police bullets because part of you has already asked and answered the question Detective when do nice kids get shot by the police

It's not that at all

And by nice I mean white

It's not that at all

Never she said

No

No the shock is not ours Detective the shock is yours and it's to be enjoyed Detective savored even for the death of my son has shocked you out of your unfeeling complacency and provided you with the opportunity to feel something real or genuine I have no doubt she said that you feel genuinely sorry for me I also have no doubt she said that the sorrow you feel feels genuinely comforting to you so instead of opportunity she said perhaps I should use the word *frisson* for this shock feels good doesn't it Detective on some real level it feels good to feel and it feels especially good to feel some connection with me some basic sympathy some primordial empathy some core narrative that we are all by

God the same and yet Detective and yet she said look at what you have to do in order to be shocked look at what you have to do in order to feel she said you have to forget you have to forget what happened last week you have to forget what happened last month and the month before that and the month before that you have to erase my past Detective and the pasts of all the people like me but you have to erase your own past too Detective your history and your blood along with my history and my blood all that erasure all that forgetting she said all that blindness she said

I wasn't there I said

It must feel good to be here though am I right two American women sitting in this nice hotel having tea you're not like those other white people are you those yahoos especially that no neck trigger happy body builder with Siberian husky eyes no Detective you care don't you you care she said about all people and maybe if you can convince me that you care enough I'll forget my bitterness and grief for just a moment and maybe give you something small some tiny glimpse into our lives some infinitesimal insight into our pain some miniscule peek into a possibility of forgiveness and you'll take that smallest image of our *dogon* mask and try to fashion some fairy tale of communication and solidarity not in order to initiate any sort of punishment for the murderer and her colleagues but in order to fabricate this bullshit myth about how we can all eventually come together if only we could forget our differences and realize that we as humans share similar desires and dreams how we're all deep down at the end of the day when the story's said and done she said really truly indisputably the same don't it just bring a tear to your eye Detective how we've all evolved from the muck of the Euphrates to the book clubbers of today and sure accidents happen and sure bad things happen to good people but these glitches these anomalies can't blind us to the fact that we share origin and biology after all we share more genetic similarities between races than within and do you know what really irritates me about that myth what really annoys me about that story she said

No I don't

The thing that really gets me is that you don't believe the story yourself she said you believe we're similar only when it suits you only when you need us to forgive you she said most of the time you're more than willing to think of us as different and by different I mean inferior your history *our* history requires that you think of us some where some how some way as different and by different I mean inferior because if you really thought we were the same if you really thought we shared a common humanity with common intellect emotions desires and fears then given the atrocities of everything from the Middle Passage to Dylan Roof to my son's murder how could you possibly face yourself how could you possibly wake up in the morning and say these are my people and we did these things to my people how could you possibly stand the knowledge of your rape murder and genocide how could you possibly face the shame of all that blood on your hands and not put a bullet in your head

I don't believe anyone is naturally inferior or superior

I still don't know what you want here she said

I want to understand something of your son I want a better picture of him than I have now

He's dead Detective that's really the only thing you can know about him now

I don't believe that I said I want to do right by him

It's too late Detective the story's over

I want to find out what really happened that night what really truly happened from different points of view not just the official story and not just your story and if there are inconsistencies or errors I want to understand these and bring them to light maybe shift the narrative a little I don't know yet

The story's already written Detective written published and sold a best seller Detective number one on the charts for two hundred and fifty years

I don't believe that

Doesn't matter what you believe Detective you're too late

I don't believe that

Why

Like I said I want to understand exactly what happened

You're not Boulder police so what are you Denver Police doing here

They wanted someone independent to oversee their investigation

And are you

Am I what

Are you independent she said

The District Attorney thinks I'm too independent

White woman shoots black man and they send a white woman to investigate that strike you as odd Detective significant

I do think there's an outcome they'd prefer I said but I like to surprise

Denver have any black detectives any detectives of color

All white women don't think alike

Have you seen my son's body yet

No I've read the coroner's report but I haven't yet viewed the body

You should look at his body Detective really look try to see

It Ain't Necessarily So
Boulderado Hotel

My son was a small boy Detective and he grew into a small man

Five seven one thirty five

He wasn't one thirty five more like one twenty five he was a slight man Detective and the police who killed him she's a strong looking woman fit probably weighs one forty herself

Maybe

He never had that growth spurt never carried much meat on his bones he wasn't sickly Detective he ran cross country and was on the ski team at Bennington he wasn't stunted or puny he was perfectly proportioned fine featured slim hipped he usually appeared she said as if he were comfortable in his skin I'm bringing this up Detective because I have a question

I'll answer if I can

So my question is this Detective what the fuck was that police afraid of

Your son was incoherent uncooperative brandishing a weapon

No Detective she was afraid from the first moment she saw him

Maybe high on drugs

He was smoking marijuana Detective if police were going to shoot everyone in Boulder who smokes dope they'd need a lot of bullets

The police officer didn't know what was happening on the other side of the door

He was with his girlfriend

She didn't know that your son had a rock a stone bookend

No Detective she was frightened from the beginning afraid the moment she walked into that room my question remains Detective why the fuck was she so frightened

Please speak a little louder

The black student population of the University of Colorado Boulder is one point nine per cent the black graduate student population is point five per cent what the fuck did she think was happening in that dorm Detective the only reason she could have acted the way she did was that she was scared utterly and absolutely frightened out of whatever wits she once possessed but I don't understand Detective I can't understand why

He knocked her down he could have killed her

So she says

I'm sorry I'm barely hearing you

She was blinded by fear Detective we don't have that luxury Detective for us terror has a face a white face

I don't know what she saw

An all too real white face well fed but unhealthy with a smooth expansive forehead and rounded almost jowly cheeks frozen blank distracted appraising blue eyes and a joyless smug thin lipped impatient Pentecostal smile we look into those unmoving unblinking unalive eyes Detective those eyes that bring nothing but pain and suffering we look into those unblinking unalive eyes and do you know what we see Detective do you know what we see in those cool blue unrippled surfaces we see black bodies Detective we see black bodies in vivid focused detail but these black bodies are never whole Detective she said these black bodies are never intact these black bodies are always twisted unnatural mutilated bent carved twisted the distortion is not from the reflection the reflection from the blue white unblinking eyes is perfect Detective like the mirrored shades of clichéd cops no the black bodies really are twisted unnatural mutilated grotesque but I'm not going to describe these bodies for you Detective these black bent twisted carved twisted black bodies you can't see them Detective you can't see them because if you could see them you would have seen them already no Detective I'm not going to describe these mutilated black twisted bodies to you but there's something you need to see something else visible in these horrific atrocious dreadful reflections do you know what that is do you know what else we can see when we look into the white blue eyes of our terror

No I said

When I look into the white blue eyes of my terror I see more white blue eyes I see that Charleston haircut his juvenile dirty blonde bowl cut with the bangs just above the eyebrows the asymmetrical slant of his face with his left ear slightly higher his wide nose and narrowed mouth thick lipped but small pinched compressed not in regret or comprehension but in complaint his eyes more green than blue all blue eyes don't look the same yes his eyes Detective green and still unabashed like the waters off

Port Comfort and his Obersalzberg cygnet neck or I see this intense stare meeting my gaze dark pupils completely surrounded by white sclera she said the tiny moustache separating the strong nose from the thin line of the mouth and the tattoo on the inner upraised forearm an undefined shape that moves my gaze upward to the finger pointing not accusatory not even angry but guiding instructing vindicated here here look here look what God hath wrought then back to the high forehead the turkey wrinkled neck white shirt with collar unbuttoned I know what the finger's indicating I've seen it before I've always seen it before one of two white verticals hovering over the horizontal line of an Indiana crowd white rags white shrouds shredded white cloth imperfectly covering bruised and lacerated black flesh the mob exuberant cheerful Detective a women with a fur collar a fur collar Detective her back to the spectacle her eyes facing the camera turned sharply to the right a tall young man in three quarters profile his hand nestled in his girl's hand his dark tie against his white shirt a ostentatious convivial grin the pleasure of being there the pleasure of being seen there dark slicked hair blending in to the black of night or other faces so many other faces Detective I've seen them all this Alabama face heavy fleshy rising indistinguishable from the neck up to the pinned ears with the forehead culminating in teased black bristled hair the features brows eyes nose mouth all crowded narrowly into the center of the caucasian face strikingly narrowed and confined the eyes shadowed by a pronounced brow ridge *Bienvenidos a Miami* a young Little Rock girl smaller than those surrounding loathing screaming hating teeth bared primordial shrieking oval O in the center of her face a hate so utterly pure a scream so utterly clear and sharp that it shatters everything the white straw hat the disdainful gaze the stylish sunglasses the childlike purse the military helmets all of it into serrated spikey fragments another face Detective another face a big man six five two ninety white white Missouri skin close cropped blonde hair outside corner of his eyes drawn down corner of his mouth drawn down as well lips eyes forehead remarkably without expression another face Detective still another face a thick Mississippi face not fat or flabby but heavy compact solid all too present visceral profuse thick neck thick chin thick lips thick nose thick eyebrows thick hair two day growth head cocked slightly to the right the eyes and mouth immobile unyielding she said or this one this face with piercing blue eyes boring out from a light Vegas tan surfer blonde hair untroubled forehead contrasted with lines around the eyes three day growth broad shoulders deep chest Baby Daddy Removal Team tee shirt or this full profile young long hair sharp nose broad shoulders forming a perfect horizontal the flag pole emerging at about three hundred and fifty degrees just slightly below the horizontal shoulders with stars and stripes attached piked thrust plunged at a black man in a suit oh say Detective can you see

    I don't know what to say

    You don't know these faces do you

    I don't know what to say I said

    I've had a long time with these faces Detective twenty

three years at least and the fear they created it wasn't an abstract fear not an amorphous invisible theoretical fear but something so real so palpable so visceral sometimes Detective she said some nights some days some nights I could feel the fear from these faces I could feel it in my chest it would course through my bloodstream through my veins and arteries my capillaries it would begin in my heart the cells of my heart the blood would carry the terror would carry the fear Detective down through the descending aorta and then through the all the capillaries that surrounded my organs my stomach my intestines my womb it would surround my stomach my guts my womb I could feel it physically feel it I could viscerally feel the fear deep in my blood flowing coursing enveloping my organs my stomach my intestines my womb moving to my extremities down my legs to my feet and toes up up through my cervix my womb my guts my stomach and heart up through the ascending aorta to my arms to my wrist my hands and the tips of my fingers then back down my arms up to my throat and into my brain the fear the terror coursing through my veins inside me filling me pounding pounding and then it would constrict Detective the fear coursing through my veins encasing my organs it would begin to constrict squeeze I would tremble Detective try to catch my breath I'd have to stop whatever I was doing it would then often settle she said this fear this terror this pain this prophecy she said just behind my eyes but it wouldn't blind me no Detective it wouldn't blind me the fear would settle behind my eyes and still I could feel it coursing through my blood vessels squeezing my lungs and heart you've never felt that fear

I worry about my son of course I do

But you don't have the faces Detective you don't have the faces and that's not all Detective sometimes she said when I'd be laughing at something a daughter said or driving to the store to get groceries I'd catch the slightest scent like the spoiled trace of last week's cenotaphic lilies that would lodge itself into the furthest darkened corner of my consciousness it was the sweetish cloying mawkish odor just on this side of perception it just was there to remind to just remind that no matter how safe we believed our family our son to be always one of those faces could wound or kill I ask you again what the fuck could that white police be afraid of

I don't know

I was thankful for the fear Detective for what pounded through my veins and flitted by my nose both warned against letting my guard down I was thankful Detective thankful for the warning but that was a mistake Detective she said we were warned but it made no difference it was all for nothing Detective all for goddam nothing we knew he was going to be killed and we did our best to protect him we did our goddam best Detective but he was killed anyway

I know and I'm sorry

Blackness requires vigilance Detective and black mothering requires something greater it's exhausting Detective absolutely irrevocably unconditionally interminably exhausting

I know and I'm sorry I said

You can't know what that's like Detective to know the fear to feel the terror to see those faces to understand the end of the story every single God damned day for twenty three years and to do everything *everything* in your power to prevent that ending we took him to the safest places we could imagine we tried to hide him in the very center none of that made the slightest difference still still the end of the story came ended like we always knew it would still still Detective he was still gunned down like a dog and yet Detective that's not the worst of it the worst of it she said that when he was killed all of my past with him twenty three years it all changed in an instant in a single moment when I learned he was shot and killed by police my entire past with him disappeared into absolute absent futility it was like I was never there it was like we never occupied the same space and time I was never there with him I never gave birth to him never held him as a newborn never kissed his always thin arms never nursed him at my breast tied his shoes dried his tears spooned his yogurt how can I live with that I can't it's one thing to kill a future Detective it's quite another to kill a past but that's what she did Detective that's what she did

I'm so sorry I said

Do you understand how unnatural it is to bury a child she said

I can almost imagine

And to know that would always be his fate

No I said

How perverted sick twisted deviate abnormal nauseating

it is to bury a son

I'm sorry

Corrupt bent degenerate invertible wretched and how you've made that perversion commonplace

I wasn't there

How can you live with yourself

I wasn't there

I don't see the faces anymore Detective

No

That's all over

No

I am dead

No I said

Yes I am dead Detective I am dead there are some things some experiences that happen to you and they change you they change the person you are you are one person before and a different person after and the person after can remember more or less the person before but Detective this is not something that has happened to me because the me no longer exists this is the one thing that could happen that I knew would destroy me as I've told you I could picture it I could imagine it I thought I could rehearse it I believed I could prepare for it but I couldn't I didn't I had that sword above my head for twenty three years and when it dropped it killed me Detective I have no past I have no future and I have no present I'm dead Detective I'm dead

I know this is hard for you

This is no metaphor Detective this is no linguistic quibble I'm not arguing over an adjective I'm dead Detective

the bullets shot by that police killed me killed my future
and my past there's nothing left Detective there's no one left
Detective the story is over everyone's dead
    You still have your daughters your husband
    Don't you dare
    I am sorry I said I'm trying to understand
    Who can understand the dead
    I don't know
    I have nothing more to say she said

Here Comes de Honey Man
Hellems Hall
University of Colorado at Boulder

Hello I'm Detective Francesca Fruscella from the Denver Police Department

What are you doing here

Thank you for inviting me into your meeting first of all I'd like you all to know how sorry I am that this young man's life was tragically cut short

She's using the passive voice

Look Bobo she's darker than you

Get out the paper bag

One eighth one sixteenth one drop I self identify

I am very sorry that this young man Johan Ratcliff was killed two nights ago here at the University of Colorado

She do the police in different voices

And as you may or may not know in Boulder County whenever a police officer is involved in the discharge of a weapon that results in loss of life the law demands an independent investigation headed by an external police officer

Why

To determine whether the lethal use of force by the police officer was justified

Your police shot an unarmed black man to death how is that justified

To determine whether that lethal use of force by said officer was justified by his or her feeling of imminent danger

Feeling what the fuck is that

Some sort of spidey sense

Fuck your feelings

Reasonable grounds for belief that the police officer or another are in imminent danger of severe bodily harm or death

We still don't know why you are here

I want to find out more about the victim what he was like who his friends were his likes and dislikes

Why

I'd like to know his story

Why

If you're investigating the killing shouldn't you be focusing on the killer

You should be back at police headquarters talking to your own

What are you really doing here

What is it you want

Maybe she wants to apologize

I'm sorry for killing your man

I'm sorry for killing your men

Police never apologize

If they did they wouldn't be police

Maybe she wants to apologize for being white

Are you sorry for being white police

Maybe she wants to apologize for being

She says she wants to understand

She says wants to understand Johan

There's nothing to understand Johan Ratcliff wasn't

killed because he carried a rock wasn't killed because he was in a dormitory at night wasn't killed because he read Kierkegaard wasn't killed because he could do some bad cab wasn't killed because he liked kush wasn't killed because he dressed like Bobby Shmurda wasn't killed because he didn't drink beer wasn't killed because he could speak Danish French and German wasn't killed because he had asthma wasn't killed because he had no jump shot wasn't killed because he didn't eat his greens wasn't killed because he always clipped his nails short wasn't killed because he preferred D'Ussé to Henny wasn't killed because he never matched his socks wasn't killed because it made him angry whenever white people would ask him what black people thought wasn't killed because he flossed twice a day wasn't killed because he hated to be cold wasn't killed because he wrote a paper using Benjamin to critique Althusser wasn't killed because he called himself Joe wasn't killed because he loved white brown black and yellow women if not equally then enthusiastically wasn't killed because he avoided swimming wasn't killed because he liked to look through his passport wasn't killed because he didn't really like old school soul wasn't killed because he loved tortilla chips with homemade salsa wasn't killed because he chose adidas over Nike wasn't killed because he didn't use the n word wasn't killed because he was really good at Halo but liked Elder Scrolls more wasn't killed because never wore a watch wasn't killed because he hated doing dishes wasn't killed because he had four different pairs of glasses wasn't killed because he wanted some nice headphones wasn't killed because he hated grocery shopping wasn't killed because he usually skipped lunch wasn't killed because he liked running in the morning wasn't killed because he could roll a clean blunt wasn't killed because he preferred Jarmusch to Lynch and Lynch to Lee wasn't killed because he wasn't on Facebook wasn't killed because he owned three Daily Paper tee shirts and two Daily Paper hoodies wasn't killed because he had never tried Vietnamese food wasn't killed because he felt ashamed when around uneducated blacks and then felt ashamed for being ashamed and then felt angry for being ashamed wasn't killed because his favorite dessert was tiramisu wasn't killed because he was into trap but worried that it was becoming too popular wasn't killed because he wasn't circumcised wasn't killed because he really liked Bernie Saunders wasn't killed because he loved Ben and Jerry's Pistachio Pistachio wasn't killed because he needed some more space from his parents wasn't killed because he disagreed with George Yancy about Christianity and black liberation wasn't killed because he didn't drive wasn't killed because he disliked professional sports wasn't killed because his natural was often lopsided wasn't killed because he freaked out on shrooms once wasn't killed because he liked Baldwin over Hurston and Hurston over Wright wasn't killed because he liked Monk over Powell and Powell over Tatum wasn't killed because he danced poorly

No none of that

You know why he was killed Detective

No

Because he was black

That's it

That's all

The police who killed him she never saw Johan Alexander Ratcliff that police she walked up the stairs opened the door and saw only black black skin black muscles black threat she walked up the stairs opened the door and looked and that single feature that one characteristic that solitary trait overshadowed all other details all other possibilities Detective she walked up the stairs opened the door and Johan Alexander Ratcliff immediately disappeared into a dark amorphous cloud of unknowable danger and when that cloud that darkness that menace came out of the doorway into that hallway what could she do what could anybody do but fire that weapon into that cloud shoot once twice three times to save herself Detective to save themselves

Pure and simple

He's dead Detective

And his death was impersonal

Indifferent

Meaningless

Like cutting off the head of a cabbage

Or drinking a glass of water

His story is over

That's the tragedy his story is finished

No more possibilities

And we wait

For the next story to finish

The next traffic stop the next shopping while black the

next loosie in the lot the next toy gun massacre the next
wrong place wrong time wrong color

    Never have to wait long
    And yet Joe's story is unique
    Irreplaceable
    Incomparable with other stories
    But we put them all into a narrative
    We erase their differences
    This is the crime you make us commit
    To bury them in a common grave
    Once again unforgiveable
    And here you are
    Sniffing around
    Forever too late
    Wanting a story
    But Joe's story is over
    If you really wanted his story
    You should have talked to him earlier
    Without clutching your purse
    Or touching your gun
    While he was still alive
    At least looked at him
    And saw someone besides a threat
    Someone besides a menace
    Someone other
    Than what you saw
    Than what you see
    Someone alive and human
    Whatever that means to you

Someone with potential
With possibilities
Without possibility a man cannot as it were draw breath
But now he can't
As it were
Draw breath
If his story is finished Detective then why are you here
Maybe she needs a career boost
I can't see how this will help her career
This won't help my career
Maybe she wants to confess
Fruscella's Italian
She's Italian right Catholic she wants to confess
I don't want to confess I wasn't there
She wants something
She wants a story
His story is finished
She wants her story
She wants her story to be
A story of her redemption
A story of her edification
A story of her education
A story of her salvation
Same old same old
You took his life now you want his story
That would be a double murder
We're not going to allow you to take his story and make
it your own
In order for you to confess you need someone to listen

To listen and forgive

We will never forgive you

There's no possible repentance nothing you can ever do can wash this away we will never forgive you

Not ever

No matter what you do

This isn't a story of racial progress

This is no history in the making

This is where history stops

That's what death means

I've nothing to confess I wasn't there

So you keep saying

We refuse you repentance we are not interested in your guilt

Your guilt Detective is besides the point

Especially since you refuse to see it

Why are you here now Detective

What are you investigating

Why are you here now

What are you doing here now 2011 you're not a child

No she's not

You notice detail Detective

That's your job

You pay attention

So why now

Why not when you were twenty why not when you were thirty why not when you were forty

It doesn't take a detective to see that police in this country have been killing black people for a long time so why now

The twenty year old could have seen it the thirty year
old could have seen it the forty year old could have seen it
The fifty year old now sees it
Why now
What do you want

I Wants to Stay Here
(A.K.A. *I Loves You Porgy*)
Hellems Hall
University of Colorado at Boulder

If you don't want to speak with me I'll go I don't want to
waste your time

We'll be happy to talk to you

Just tell us what you want

Why you are here

The way we see it is that you see your problems as
both epistemological and judicial you want to know what
happened that's the epistemological and you want to apply
what you know to the judicial to the distributive procedural
retributive restorative and we don't see this as either
epistemological or judicial as for epistemological we know
what happened you know what happened someone called
the police on a black man a student whose presence was
perfectly unassailably unequivocally both reasonable and
appropriate he was a student he was invited he was unarmed
he belonged there by any stretch of the imagination

He was high uncooperative and he attacked the police
officer

And yet he was murdered there by a member of the
police who was called to keep the peace

He had a rock a large stone

Your initial objections change nothing if he was
high so what that's not a capital crime same with being
uncooperative no white kid gets shot for that as for the

alleged attack isn't that how you talk we believe you have your doubts regarding that no if you were certain your police was attacked we don't think you'd be here so no we don't think this is an epistemological problem

You know what happened

We know what happened

Knowledge is not the problem

The second problem you face is judicial the distributive aspect suggests that justice be distributed across society fairly and equitably on the surface this appears important but we both know to insist on the distributive here and now with a white cop and a black victim is a fool's errand the second is the procedural which is what police stories usually focus on all that forensic evidence with fiber strands spectrum cameras microscopes ballistics DNA samples but we know the killer we've always known the killer we've always known who done it and why retributive is a funny one it depends on how you read your Old Testament an eye for an eye and a tooth for a tooth on the one hand it means that criminals need to be disciplined society's civility depends on punishment as a deterrent if you as a citizen transgress the law then you as a citizen deserve punishment it also means at the same time that the punishment should fit the crime should never exceed the crime so if someone takes your eye then you can only take their eye you aren't allowed to take both their eyes or kill them

Like the Godfather said that is not justice your daughter is still alive

Another story of police failure

We don't want retribution

How can you retribute genocide you can't
You can ask the Ratcliff family
But even if that police was put away
Johan Alexander Ratcliff would still be dead
Retribution is a tired narrative
Hollywood myth notwithstanding
And finally there's the restorative
The biggest joke of all
Can't dialogue the dead
The conversation would be a trifle one sided
Like we said Johan Alexander Ratcliff and his family
will never be restored
And neither will this community
But I do think it's why you're here
You want to restore
You want to restore your wounded community we were
injured but we can heal we shall overcome
Some day
Our man is killed and you're the one in pain
And it's your job to restore balance
Your sense of self
This is the true job of the police
Restore the story
The story of an idyllic safe inclusive prosperous educat-
ed liberal community who's threatened one day by an un-
cooperative drugged inappropriate dark other and a white
fit but small woman always in danger of imminent bodily
harm arrives to keep everybody safe and sound but things
get out of hand she's attacked and responds with deadly

force it's a tragedy yes but who can blame her the community is shocked destabilized undermined and you come in from outside Detective from big city Denver a woman with uncertain or at least flexible sympathies you come in another white woman on a rescue mission to reassure us all finally that the incident while regrettable and even unavoidable was not unspeakable and inconsequential no we all can must learn from this sad and tragic death we can mourn together and truly come together to create a new and diverse community fulfilling the promise of our democracy that's the restoration you're interested in

U S A U S A

That's the justice you desire

You desire to reestablish stability

Reinscribe the status quo

The thing is the status quo was rotten in the first place

The status quo got us killed

We don't want that justice

That justice gets us killed

Damned if I do and damned if I don't

Oh don't feel sorry for yourself Detective

This is not about you

If you don't want justice what do you want

We want you to stop shooting us

What is it you say put your weapon down

Then we can talk

No this is not a question of epistemology or of justice

What is it then

A question of ethics and aesthetics Detective

I have no idea what you're talking about

And of time

This ventriloquism is absurd

Look Detective we're not trying to teach you anything

You came to us wanting a story

We're trying to give you a new story

Or at least tell you the ones you need to avoid

The story of guilt and innocence

The story of self and other

Avoid

You keep insisting on your innocence Detective as if guilt depended on physical presence

On being there

On pulling the trigger

We are not speaking of guilt or rather we are not speaking only of guilt we know you are a police and trained to think in terms of either or guilt or not guilt which is never the same thing as innocence but we are not primarily interested in your guilt or any one person's guilt Detective guilt implies the possibility of payment through repentance or pecuniary compensation guilt implies justice and we refuse that clichéd story arc there's nothing you or anyone can do Detective to assuage your guilt we think that's why you're here and by here I mean this whole narrative to assuage your guilt for all those years of not paying enough attention

I wasn't there I didn't do anything I'm just trying to find out the truth

Guilt is easy cheap self indulgent feeling guilty is its own compensation guilt implies forgiveness don't you think if you ask for forgiveness it's inexcusable or at least churlish of us to refuse but we do refuse the whole guilt story no we're not at all interested in your cut rate dime store bargain bin sentiment or lack thereof

If you need to feel guilt feel collective guilt Detective

Which is another way of saying shame

Shame can't be erased can't be expunged can't be cleansed through uncountable Hail Mary's weekends at the food bank or reading Toni Morrison no shame is what you can't scrub out even with lye bleach and hard soap shame is always there Detective you can't apologize your way out of it shame has nothing to do with what you've done and everything to do with what you are

If you were born here you were born with shame shame is the default and innocence the perversion the United States' original originating first sin is chattel slavery your forebears didn't have to own slaves for you to be complicit you don't have to knot the rope to be part of the lynch mob the problem with usual thinking about guilt and innocence is that they quickly become internal narratives they quickly become primal psychological stories of the self if you're convinced you're innocent you're home free and if you think you're guilty you say you're sorry and that's it you don't really do anything when you're innocent and when you're guilty you're interested only in your own exculpation nothing happens with either guilt or innocence and without action where's the story we need to get beyond that

In my world innocence and guilt are paramount if you're innocent you go free and if you're guilty and we can prove it you're punished pretty fucking important I'd say

This isn't your world Detective or it is and that's the problem

She do the police in different voices

Nothing to see here

No mystery

No procedural

No epiphany

White people don't like thinking of hereditary sin collective guilt or shame goes against every story you tell yourself about this country if you ignore collective guilt then individually you can be as innocent as snow

We call it the racists back then syndrome

The I have black friends syndrome

The I don't see color syndrome

Self and other

Same and different

Another hard one

Another system buried deep in our thinking

From the ancient Greeks *politēs* and *barbaros*

I hate to be that guy in the glasses who always brings up Hegel

To today good people and those people

But Hegel

That thinking is dangerous it's the most dangerous thinking there is

And it's really hard to shake

If you think of black people in terms of self and other you're caught in this dilemma this American dilemma if we are at ground human the same a part of you then how can you do the things you do to us and live with yourselves if we are really like you and identify with you then you've committed brutal relentless violence against yourself and that's the symptom of a desperate and terminal sickness but if we are totally foreign if we are completely other to you different like cattle or sheep then you can do anything you want to us murder rape lynch no problem but you don't can't quite believe that we are totally different completely inhuman given our singing dancing and writing so we are neither other to you nor the same and you can't process this so you've developed this elaborate continuum between self and other a sliding scale as it were and you slide it back and forth at will sometimes our physical gestures when we get out of a car too quickly reach for our wallets or pull our hoodies over our heads we're foreign animal like frightening sinister but other times when we cook food you eat write books you read make films you see we're human with similar desires and fears similar wishes for our children similar hopes and dreams

And how you love watching us watching our bodies watching our bodies dance sing play ball our innate rhythm and our fast twitch muscles are exquisite if only your bodies could move like that but you're not looking in a mirror are you when Beyoncé jitterbugs or Lebron dunks you're not looking in a mirror when Serena serves or Misty swans you're somehow not proud of this human accomplishment you don't desire to share this beauty no you separate yourself from it you feel cheated envious somehow belittled and you compensate with labels lacking intelligence sex crazed shut up and dribble just because she's black

So which is it

Are we the same or are we different

You can't decide and yet you need to decide this perpetual deciding is basic fundamental essential to you you make it anytime you come into contact with us what degree of humanity will you grant us at any given moment it must be exhausting for you

It's exhausting for us

And you have so many others and so many other decisions brown people red people yellow people Jews women gay lesbian trans

And all this deciding spreads like cancer

We're not immune no one is

The thing is you depend on us Detective you need us without us you wouldn't be you

We are not your replacement

We are not your negation

We are both other and the same

At the same time

In time

And by in time I don't mean in the future or only in the future

Patience is no longer a virtue

No matter what you think we're not born black just as you're not born white we have to learn what all this means through experience and unlearn it as well with imagination we all have to become who we are in time

We are multitudes

You need to let go of thinking like the police

You need new genres Detective new clues new ways of being new beauties new conceivable choices where guilt isn't individual where the other isn't sacrificed where nothing is restored where we don't get killed by police think of the freedom Detective where there's more than one solution where the imagination isn't shackled where there are truly multiple possibilities this is what aesthetics means the freedom to choose wisely and well the freedom to make oneself new over and over again

    I'm confused I've no idea what you're talking about
    And ethics means can you take responsibility
    To let the other be
    Can you love us
    Without knowing us
    Can you love us
    Without judging us
    Can you love us
    Without looking in the mirror
    Can you love us
    And let us *be*
    Maybe you just need to sit down for a few
    Sit down and listen

There's a Boat That's Leaving Soon for New York

Detective Francesca Fruscella was released from the Boulder County Critical Incident Team Friday December 4th and was ordered to turn in her files notes and any documents or materials relating to the case to the Boulder District Attorney's Office the case was never mentioned by her Denver superiors.

On March 7th 2012 the Boulder District Attorney announced that no charges would be filed against Officer Darcy Shields in the shooting death of Johan Alexander Ratcliff the Boulder Police Department in a separate communication indicated that no disciplinary action would be forthcoming against Shields who is presently an officer in good standing of the Boulder Police Department.

JEFFREY DeSHELL has published eight novels, most recently *Masses and Motets* in 2019. He was a Fulbright Teaching Fellow in Budapest, and has taught in Northern Cyprus, the American Midwest and Bard College. Currently he is a Professor of English at the University of Colorado at Boulder. He splits his time between Boulder and upstate NY, with the novelist Elisabeth Sheffield and their twin boys.

jeffreydeshell.net

www.ingramcontent.com/pod-product-compliance
Lightning Source LLC
Chambersburg PA
CBHW011202190726
48286CB00009B/2879